I0598654

The Collected Hilary Long Mysteries

Part 1

by

Margaret Cooper Evans

First Published by Nuova Stella (publishing)
2017

Copyright 2014-2017 © Margaret Cooper-Evans
Covers by Andrew Evans
ISBN: 0-9934068-1-5
ISBN-13: 978-0-9934068-1-2

With thanks to

Andrew Evans for his support, proof reading and book cover design.

Jean Kilford for her continued encouragement.

Sue Davies and The Adderbury Morris for inspiring Summertime in Overdown

And the National Trust who allow me to patrol their Historic Houses and sometimes meet the people who owned them.

CONTENTS

Contains special new illustrations

The Maps of Overdown

and Novelettes

Upside down in Overdown

Summertime in Overdown

plus the previously unpublished short story:

The Girl in the Louboutin Shoes

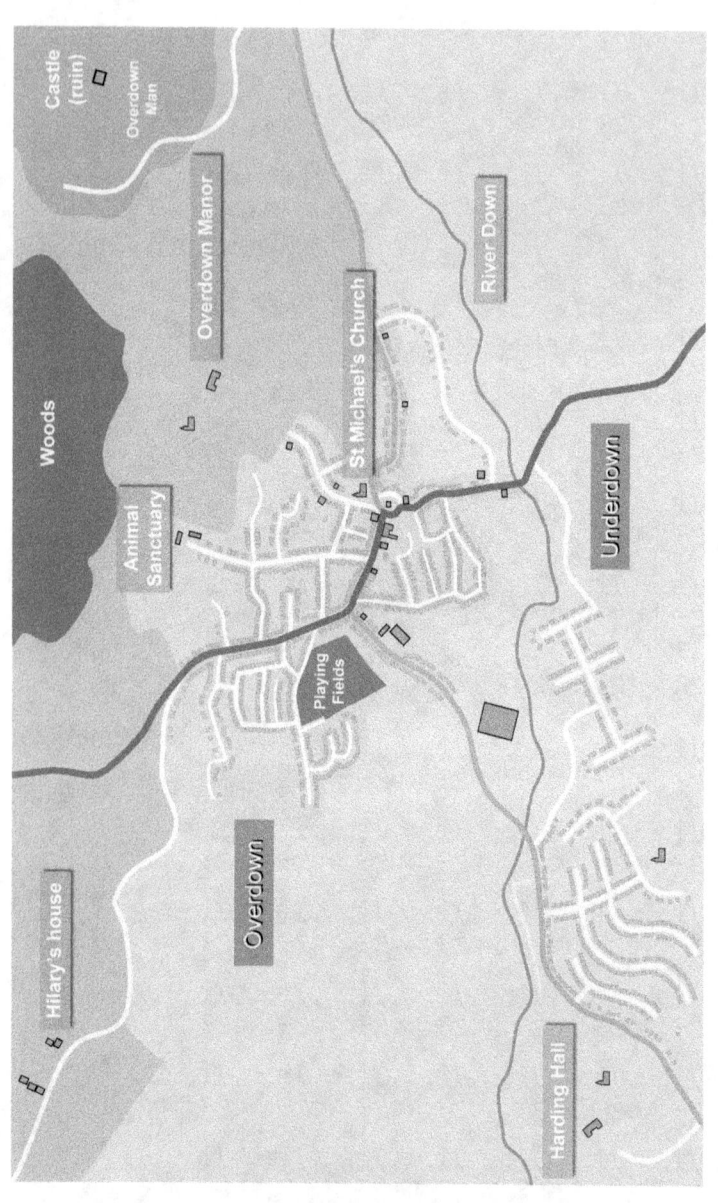

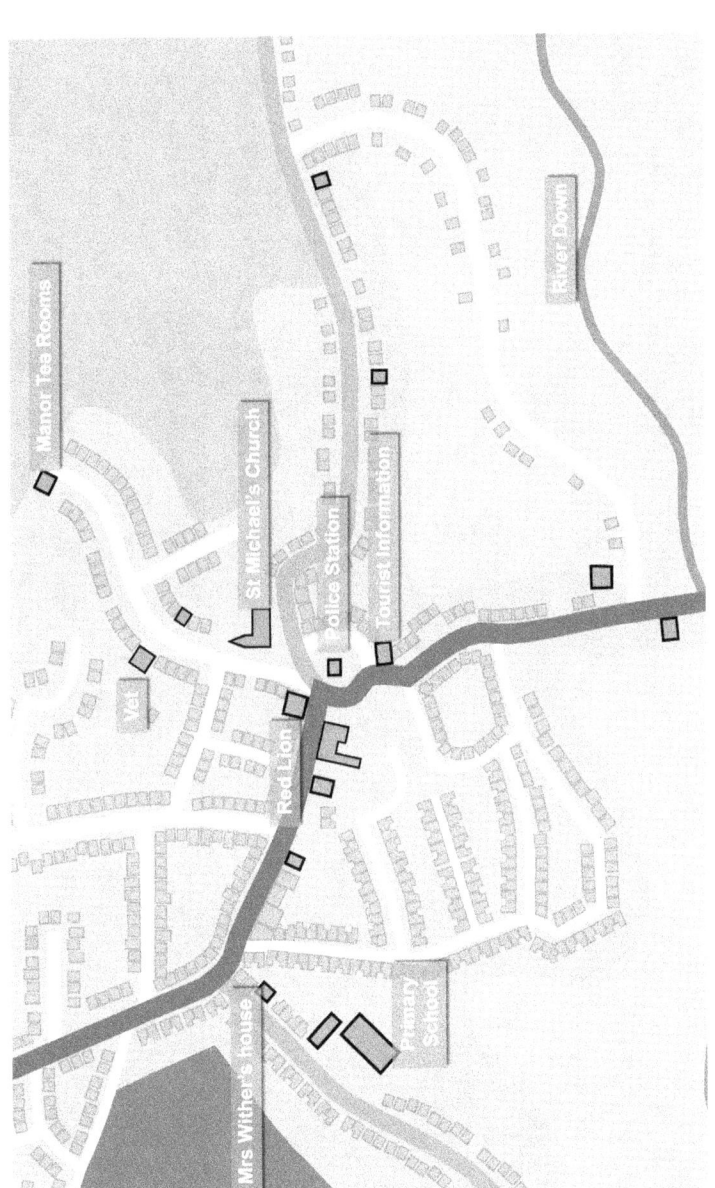

Upside down in Overdown

I sat for a long time in my expensive Cadogan Square flat thinking about the name I should choose. I didn't normally watch TV during the daytime, but I thought I'd take the first name from the first person I saw, who just happened to be a television doctor, so Hilary was randomly chosen as my first name.

What next? I thought, staring at the white marble mantelpiece forever. It has to be believable. Ordinary. I thought of Hilary Mantel, but a quick check on my iPhone revealed it was already taken. I really must read more.

I had been thinking for a very long time about what I was going to do, and without further inspiration Hilary Long was born.

So here I am now, in a little cottage, in a little Cotswold village called Overdown.

Overdown because it overlooks the beautiful hillsides surrounding it known locally as 'the Downs'. I don't know why I chose here, I could have gone anywhere in the world.

But I wanted to find a place and make it mine, and I had driven through the Cotswolds many times and wondered what it would be like to live in one of the old yellow stone cottages set in the picturesque landscape. I thought it was somewhere I could rest and regroup.

The cottage was cold damp and neglected when I paid cash for it from a dapper relative of the person who had lived there. So I took it over. It was cheap because of the state it was in, and slowly over the past few months I had the adventure of making it habitable.

I started with lighting a fire in the grate, closely followed by calling the chimney sweep when flames popped out of the top of the chimney and a roasted crow and it's nest fell into the fireplace.

Disappearing is easier than you might think.

Frankly, I'd had enough. Enough of work, enough of relationships, enough of everything and especially enough of being me. I used to be nice, too nice at work. Became very successful and then I became ruthless, a really horrible person, and one day the nice side of me had an epiphany and I decided it had to stop. I decided to take a holiday from myself.

I looked over the darkening hillside and lights were starting to twinkle in the cottages sprinkled across the downs.

Warm orange glows that spelt dinner and conversation and a fireside with logs in the grate and big comfy armchairs. Children fighting over the TV remote or their games or doing their homework. The smell of hot food from the kitchen.

I drew the curtains leaving the centre of the window so I could see the view, lit my new wood burning stove, put on a couple of table lamps and went into my newly fitted kitchen and put a garlic chicken with small potatoes ready meal into one of the ovens of my new range cooker.

I smiled at how you can get anything you want at any time of year now.

Like new potatoes in the autumn.

I did miss good conversation, I had actually started to miss work, but as I didn't exist any more in that world, going back wasn't an option. I had well and truly burnt my bridges.

It hurt very much, but leaving has done me more good than staying ever would have. Sometimes I see their faces in my sleep and have to turn my mind off by listening to music. Nothing that reminds me of anything. My childhood, my teenage years, my young womanhood. So I listen to obscure classical music that makes me grate my teeth at times but stops me thinking.

I might get a cat or a dog, I'm not sure.

I eat my dinner with a glass of Bergerac sec from the supermarket and stare out at the darkened view and my overgrown garden. I have a gardener coming on Monday, so it will look better soon.

It's been a long time since my disappearance was on the News. Months now.

They've all forgotten about me so quickly. No yellow ribbons round oak trees for me, once a sign to welcome prisoners home now a generic welcome back for anyone who goes missing. I did read my Obit in the Times and I didn't even come out of that very well. Shows you what a horrible person I must have been. I wasn't missed, all finished now, a new start, don't think about it.

That was delicious, the garlic chicken melted in my mouth and the baby new roasted potatoes and carrots were superb. I got out some Irish cream liqueur ice cream. Not being the only woman in the world who loves Baileys in every form I can't be traced by that!

I kept one photo of who I was, just one. So I remember. So when I'm old they will know, when they find it, they'll know who I really was.

I think I'll join the church. No. The WI ? The dog walkers club?

Dog or cat? With that in mind I climbed the brand new oak staircase to my bedroom at the back of the house, undressed and like a zombie staggered to my bed and was asleep in a second.

I woke up to a loud banging on the front door, how is it no-one ever sees the new electric doorbell? God, have I overslept? Is that the gardener guy already? Is it 9 o'clock?

It's not 9am it's half past six, I rush to the front window and glimpse police at my front door, and my heart pounds so loudly that I'm sure they can hear it. "Hang on." I shout out of the front window, my glasses are on squoinky and my hair is a mess.

Two policemen who look young enough to be my sons look up at me with their scrubbed fresh faces.

"Mrs Long?" one asks.

"Miss" I correct him sticking to my lie. "What's the problem?" I ask trying to pull my fleece over my head.

"This." The other young policeman stands back, and I see the shape of the vicar lying face down in the long grass, almost covered by weeds, long sticky buds are in his hair.

I can't help but throw up out of the window and pretty soon two nice young men are covered in an avalanche of diced carrot.

"Sorry. Sorry." I gulp, wiping my hand across my lips. I shut the window and rush downstairs grabbing some kitchen towel off the new kitchen worktop.

It's black granite with mica and it sparkles I like that.

As I open the door the two young men stare at men. I can't work out if they are angry or not.

"Here." I shove yards of kitchen towel at them. "Come in there's a sink in the downstairs toilet."

They walk into my newly painted hallway. "Do you want me to call anyone?" I pick up the phone.

I'm pleased to see the dark haired one laughing as he runs his flat cap under the tap. "No, we just saw the vicar as we were passing. Well we saw his feet sticking out onto the path and thought it might be a drunk, we've called forensics and an ambulance."

"Oh God." I say dramatically.

"Did you know him well?" asked the fair shaven headed policeman as he dried off his left shoulder.

"No, not at all." I flopped in the chair by the table. "It's just that I've got a gardener coming at 9 and now I don't know what to do, the grass can't be cut now can it?"

They both laughed. "No, we have to wait for forensics to come, he probably walked up to welcome you to the village and had a heart attack in your garden."

"So I killed the vicar? Oh no, poor man." I put my head in my hands, this was weird and I didn't like it. The clock struck 7, "I'll go and get dressed, I need a shower, is that ok?" I pointed to my smart red kettle, "Make yourself tea or coffee if you want."

I raced upstairs into the bathroom remembering that I couldn't stalk naked face across the top landing from the shower to get my clothes this morning. I picked out a sensible skirt and a matching olive green jumper, grabbed my underwear and tights and went to have my shower.

I kept the door open a crack, I wanted to hear what they were saying.

As he was talking I could hear the dark haired one walking about picking up this and that. I made sure there was nothing anywhere to give me away – they would find nothing. My photo was in my box at the bank.

I turned my back to the door to shower my face and I thought I heard a floorboard creak on the landing. I didn't look round. I dressed as quickly as I could and brushed my shoulder length dark hair which was now lank and wet put on my big black glasses and went downstairs.

"I'm Constable Constable." the dark one laughed, "James, and yes I am related to the painter."

"PC Derek Lowndes" said the other one.

"Hilary Long, but you know that don't you?" I asked.

"Your car, checked the plates, routine." PC Constable said as he handed me a tea.

"Oh." I said taking a sip of the tea which was surprisingly ok.

Well, it was a lost morning. So many questions, turning my lovely blond, muscular gardener called Toby away, the ambulance, the forensics team.

All I could think of was why me? Why did this happen to me?

The local news turned up, so I hid in my dilapidated shed, Constable Constable came to get me to make a statement. The time I went to bed. No I didn't hear anything, first I knew was when the police were hammering at my door. So many people in and around my house, I hated it. This was not what I ran away to do. I was supposed to be living a quiet normal life, away from everything – not back in the thick of things.

By four o'clock the day was done and so was I. Bloody vicar, not a mark on him apparently, hadn't been drinking, but he had been lying there in my garden, unbeknownst to me, all night. He had snail trails all over his dark suit, possibly lying there in the pitch black while I ate my dinner and stared at the view.

I washed and brushed my hair, tidied up my new little house. A dog, I thought, a dog would have barked at someone in the garden. I made up my mind to get a dog.

A big dog. A VERY big dog.

I sat with a glass of wine, and yes four o'clock in the afternoon is early, but it had been a hell of a day. I kicked off my sensible shoes and was just sinking into my shabby chic sofa when there was a knock at the door.

Now what? I thought as I pushed the glass behind the table lamp. I didn't want anyone to think I was an alcoholic. That wasn't part of my plan.

Neither was what happened next.

"Hello", he stood tall dark and handsome in well cut jeans and a trendy tee shirt.

"Constable Constable." I blathered staring at him.

"I came to see if you were all right." he smiled.

"I'm very pissed off, I didn't have that sort of day planned, guess the vicar didn't either."

His eyes softened and he gave me a bunch of flowers, and not from the local garage, he'd hidden them behind his back. "For you" he smiled.

He had a broad friendly smile set in a handsome face, brown eyes, his black hair brushed off his forehead.

"But I spewed up on you." I stuttered.

"Hills, may I call you Hills?"

"Okay.. " I elongated the word, "if you must."

I really must get a very big dog, I thought to myself. He moved closer to me and gave me a very sexy look, I looked behind me into the passageway just in case – but no, he was actually looking at me.

He followed me into the kitchen as I took the flowers through and poured water into my new butlers sink, so deep and so cold. I love butlers sinks don't you? I popped the flowers into the water and turned to find him very very close to me. His aftershave was expensive and fresh like him. Not the expensive bit but you got that? Right?

"You're not who you pretend to be." He smiled at me. "Are you?"

I squeezed away from him as he'd squashed me against the sink. "Call me Jamie."

"Call me confused." I stared at him.

"I saw you." He smiled at me his eyes half closed, "the real you, in the shower, your beautiful long legs, your trim little waist, your long dark hair.

Your skin is the colour of pale corn in the summer, so lovely. The pretty lace underwear, black wasn't it?" He stroked my face, took off my glasses and kissed me on the lips. Soft firm lingering.

"What the hell are you doing?" I pushed him off, but I liked the kiss, I hadn't been kissed like that for what seemed like an age.

"Sorry." he smiled, I knew he wasn't. "But you're going to waste away up here on this hill." he sat on my spot on the sofa, strangely I was afraid of him finding my glass of wine tucked behind the lamp. Think fast, think fast, but my story fell out of my head and I couldn't remember a thing.

"I don't know what you're doing." I said eventually.

"What are you doing?" he asked, "more to the point." he picked up the wine glass and sipped it running his tongue across the rim my lips had touched.

The story came back to me in floods. "Hiding away." I sat next to him.

"Trying to keep out of the limelight."

"Why?" he finished the glass.

"You'll laugh at me." I lowered my eyes.

"I won't." He took my hand and kissed it. "Tell me."

"I won the lottery." I lied, "I thought I could buy peace and quiet move away from the city, from the Library where I worked, it was all going well until this afternoon." I'm getting good at this lying lark I thought to myself.

I really must get an Alsatian or perhaps a noisy yappy dog, or both.

He stared at me and smiled, he took my hands in his, "So that's why you changed your name and only came into being a few months ago."

"Yes." I whispered, he'd looked me up. Scary.

"Thank you." he held my hands for what seemed an age. "Are you really 40?"

"No 33, but that's bad enough." I smiled.

"No family?" he asked.

"None that care other than for the money." I stood up, "So I pretty much please myself." he still had hold of my hands which were getting a bit clammy now.

"What is all this about officer? A strange sort of investigation." I looked him up and down, "Plain but expensive clothes?" I joked.

He stood up. "Upstairs?" he smiled tracing his fingers under my blouse and across the lace of my bra, my deprived (or is it depraved) loins said yes, but my head said no.

"No," I said firmly "just because I chucked up on you doesn't mean you can take advantage of me."

"You're feisty." he grinned. "I like that. Lets start again, can I take you out for a drink?"

"I'm older than you." I smiled wanting to kiss his face off.

"Is that a yes?" he grinned.

"Yes." I said as we walked to the door. He bent and kissed me chastely on the lips. The wooden front door slammed shut.

Fuck Fuck Fuck I thought what have I done?

That door badly needs a coat of paint – I thought - I'll put it on my to do list.

That night in my dreams I was the person I used to be. In my arms a young muscular man, on my body a blood red silk negligee, my painted toenails and fingernails the same colour as my lingerie. Champagne glasses sparkled gold at the side of the bed, the sheets gold expensive embroidered silk.

A white dog came into the room and snarled at me. I woke with a start sweating. What did it mean?

Next morning I turned the TV news on. Lots about the Vicar, a decorated Falklands war hero, married happily for years to the Lady of the Manor.

Everyone in the village was shocked. Me more so, seeing the dreadful state of my front garden on the local news.

I looked out of the front window, there was still yellow and black police tape all over the garden.

I showered and dressed trying to process the events of the previous night. I let my guard down, got confused, it wasn't going to happen again. One thing I'd learnt from my old life was that you don't cross the police, and you don't necessarily trust them either. Jamie was a creep I decided, but I had to keep him on side.

I locked the door behind me and stood for a moment looking at the Vicar shaped dent in my overgrown lawn. I saw Toby walking up the lane from his battered van, hands in his jeans pockets.

"Can't do it yet then." he looked at the grass and the yellow and black tape all around my dry stone wall and the path to the house. "No," I put my hand on the wooden gate, "Not until they tell me I can – sorry."

"I can start on the back if you like." he suggested, "Cut back the overgrowth, cut the grass."

"Yes," I smiled at him "do that, it'll cheer me up, I feel a bit sick looking at that." I pointed to the Vicar dent in the grass, "I'll be glad when you can get rid of it."

"Are they coming back?" Toby asked.

"I don't know." I smiled at him. "I threw up on the two policemen who discovered it. - By accident." I added quickly, "I was leaning out of the top window, saw the Vicar and before I knew what happened I had two cops covered in diced carrot."

He laughed, "So you'll be wanting me to hose down the porch roof and the path then."

"Thanks." I gave him the spare key. "Make yourself some tea or coffee or there's cold drinks in the fridge." I thought for a second, "Do you know James Constable?"

"Not really, he went to public school, I went to the local comp." he walked back to his van and me to my car. "He won't be a PC for very long his Dad knows all the important people in Overdown, he'll be out of here by the end of the year."

I put my keys in my car door. "I don't like him."

"Fair enough missus." Toby smiled, "where are you off to?"

"Little Stocking, I hear there's a rescue centre there." I got in the car and put the name in the SatNav.

Toby leant on the window of the car, "Don't take the first turn the SatNav gives you – it's the second turn out of the village – the first turn will take you up to the manor house and there'll be enough going on there today."

"How far away is it?" I asked wondering how far the poor Vicar had walked.

"About three miles." he pointed down the road.

"Thanks," I turned the key in my little car and drove down the hill, the landscape widened into lush corn filled fields golden in the early morning sun. Fluffy green trees and hedges framed the side of the road.

It was late summer and although the nights would be drawing in soon, the days were still very warm. It was coming to the end of August. I had spent so much time working on the cottage, driving to and from the B&Q at Tetbury. Seeing to builders and kitchen fitters that I hadn't actually had time to go into Overdown or to appreciate much else to about where I had chosen to live, apart from the view from my lounge window. I had missed a glorious hot summer in a frenzy of DIY.

I drove past the first turning, the drive up to the Manor, there were police cars on the drive and an incident support unit van.

Pennies started to drop with alarming regularity. Firstly why didn't Mrs Vicar miss her husband and report him? Why did Mr Vicar decide to go and see someone he'd never met before and walk three miles uphill in the dark to do it? Most of all – yes most of all why were there no footsteps in the long grass up to where he was lying? It looked to me as if he'd been thrown over the garden wall when I first saw his shape in the grass.

Even this morning I noticed that the footsteps around the shape to lift him off and the wheel marks of the stretcher did not go over where he should have walked to fall there.

I swerved to avoid a bright red Mercedes hurtling down the road towards me.

I turned into the rescue centre where dogs barked and cats mewed. I parked up and went into the Reception, I was soon walking along a row of cages and saw a small white terrier with a brown patch on his back, he was chasing a ball around on his own, as soon as he came up to me I knew he was the one.

He had a brown patch across his top lips that looked like a moustache, and had very intelligent brown eyes. I read the label on his cage. "Hello Poirot." I smiled stroking his head, he's obviously been called Poirot for his neat little tashe. He rubbed his face on my hand and stood up on his short stubby back legs to try to get nearer to me.

About half past two having spent all morning at the re-homing centre signing forms and agreeing to home visits, I drove back to my cottage with a small brown and white terrier called Poirot and a silver tabby kitten I intended to call Miss Marple in two boxes in the back of the car. Well, it had to be done in view of the circumstances!

When I arrived home, Constable Constable and Constable Lowndes were waiting on my doorstep.

"Where have you been?" PC Lowndes asked, "we've been trying to get hold of you all day."

"To the rescue centre." I smiled slightly worried as I lifted Poirot and Miss Marples boxes out of my car unaided.

"What's happened?" I asked, knowing immediately what the answer would be.

"The Reverend Hart was murdered." Jamie said seriously.

"Oh my God." I said with pretend shock. "But I don't understand."

"The post-mortem found his stomach was lacerated and he had arsenic poisoning."

"So why are you here?" I asked, "I've only been in the village a few months and I don't know anyone here. I didn't even know the Vicar's name until you said it a moment ago."

"He was in your front garden." PC Lowndes said. " We have to ask you why."

"I don't know," I said struggling up the path with a cat and dog box, my handbag and my car keys, "why would you think I would ?"

I put the boxes on top of one another and unlocked the front door, I put the boxes on my newly laid quarry tiled kitchen floor and the policemen followed me in.

"As far as I know anyone could have driven him up here and thrown him over the wall." I said giving as many clues as I could without sounding as if I knew anything.

"Wouldn't you have heard it?" he asked.

"I sleep in the back." I said, "Come and look."

They followed me upstairs and my back bedroom was as usual immaculate.

Bed made, wardrobe closed. I took them to the smaller front bedroom it was full of moving boxes waiting to be unpacked, curtains to be put up and pots of paint waiting to be used.

"So you heard nothing ?" PC Constable asked.

"No. I thought I told you all this yesterday, I moved to this village for peace and quiet, not for all of this." I was starting to get tetchy, "look I've got two rescue animals I need to settle in."

"All right," PC Lowndes smiled kindly, "it must be very difficult all of this."

"I just want to be left alone, cut the front lawn, plant some roses, have my pets, some peace and quiet and look at the view."

As I opened the door for them I looked over the rolling hills. Underdown village was in the lea of the valley. The roads wound through the waving fields of corn,and the trees were rustling in the warm breeze, it could have been a lovely place to live, but already I was thinking of leaving.

Constable Constable hung back and popped his head round the door.

"9.o'clock Red Lion." he whispered.

I said nothing as I closed the door behind him. I kicked off my shoes and opened the boxes to welcome my new little pets to their new little home.

Well 9.o'clock came and went, and I was painting the back door, well just finished, and was about to wash the brushes out when there was a loud knock at the door. Why doesn't anyone see my doorbell?

I didn't need to answer it. Someone else did it for me. I washed my hands and walked into the lounge.

Miss Marple was asleep on a cushion and Poirot was growling at Constable Constable.

"What are you doing here mam?" the young PC asked his Chief Constable.

The surprise on his face and the way he stuttered the question made me realise I had done the right thing.

"Christine is an old friend." I smiled I bumped into her the other day on the way back from the pet rescue centre." Lying was coming so easily to me now that I was surprising myself.

The tall blonde woman about my age spoke.

"James Constable." A smile flickered across her tanned beautiful face, she was tough and it showed. "What do you think you are doing? "

"Well I.." he stuttered.

She waved a finger at him. "No, no, no, James, you do not" putting a strong emphasis on the not, "commit crimes, you prevent them."

"Commit crimes?" he looked puzzled.

"Sexual assault, searching without a warrant, need I go on? "She smiled brushing a stray wisp of her blonde bob behind her ear with her well manicured finger.

"What? What?" he looked embarrassed and flushed red from the collar up, clearly trying to get a grip on himself. "What happens next?"

"Nothing, Miss Long will not press charges if you leave her alone, I'll see you out James."

At the door I heard her whisper, "How could you be so stupid?"

The door clicked shut after him.

"Thank you," I smiled at her.

"What for?" she asked picking up her stylish pale blue wool coat and putting it on.

"Believing me." I leant on the door frame as I saw her out, looking at the view, the stars twinkled overhead matching the lights in the cottages in Underdown.

"Well, I know James of old, he's over enthusiastic in many ways, perhaps he thought he was on to something that would crack the case." She looked sadly at the dark imprint in the grass, but it was so dark even the light from my cottage door did not illuminate it properly.

"Hardly." I said bitterly, "I just wanted a bit of peace and quiet, go shopping for my new house, enjoy my pets and the view, but I guess I'll have to sell it now."

"Why?" she asked taking her car keys out of her coat pocket.

"Because my garden and that shape in it has become a tourist attraction."

I stared at the pressed grass under the black and yellow tape, "I'll always remember the morning I woke up and saw the Vicar there."

"It's time for Richard to go," she said sadly, "I'll get Toby to come tomorrow and mow it for you, lets get rid of the memories." She held my wrist as she left, "If you need to see a counsellor we can arrange that for you." There was a strange break in her voice as if it was she, and not me, who needed help.

"Thank you, but no." I watched her walk to her BMW, she got in and turned the lights on. As I heard the car engine purr into life I closed my front door.

I awoke the following morning to Toby hammering on my door.

"Hilary, Hilary." he shouted, "Miss Long."

I opened the door and in the same spot as the Vicar had been, lay Christine West, Chief of Police. She had been shot in the head, her lovely pale blue coat turning purple with her blood. I stared at her open blue eyes, her immaculate blonde bob matted with clotted blood. My knees crumpled and the next thing I remember was that I was back in my own bed with my little pets at my feet and a cup of hot sweet tea on my side table.

I looked up and there was James Constable.

"You." I sat up ready to bolt.

"No." he looked sad, "Christine was my father's wife, I'd never do that to her, or anyone." he added quickly. "I don't think this is connected to the Vicar's murder."

"Why me? Why this house?" I clutched my duvet to my chest.

James sat on the edge of the bed making me feel uncomfortable. "This house had been derelict for years, even when the last owner lived here. It was left empty for about eight years after he died while the solicitor found his next of kin – the person you bought it from."

Toby appeared at the door, "I'm going missus, can't do anything today, the place is crawling with police again. No offence James."

"None taken." James saw PC Lowndes in the doorway as Toby started to leave.

"Witnesses?" I said quickly. "Any witnesses?"

"Not yet," PC Lowndes came in, "But we don't think it's you – it would be strange to pile bodies up on your own doorstep and not run away."

My old life was starting to seem like a good option, at least there were no murders in it yet. "Toby!" I called downstairs not sure if he could hear me or if he was already out of the door.

"Yes missus," his voice came up the stairs.

"Can you take my cat and dog for a day or two ? I'll pay you. I just need to get away from here."

"Surely." came his voice and he thundered up the stairs put an animal under each arm and took them to his van.

"Where are you going?" PC Lowndes asked.

"I'm going to visit a friend for a few days, I can't ask her here she might end up dead in the front garden. Is that ok with you lot?"

The two policemen looked at each other. "Yes." they answered together.

They stood up and left thundering down my new oak staircase. I walked to the spare room and glimpsed through the curtains, there was a huge yellow and blue tent in my front garden now, with people in white paper suits searching the long grass with their fingers.

Fuck this, I thought when the house was empty, these people are useless, time to go back to being me for a while.

I arrived in Bath after about an hour, I booked into my usual Georgian Hotel under my old name. No one asked anything, they knew me so well, I doubt if they even realised I'd gone missing a few months ago.

In the elegantly furnished room I threw my cases onto the bed and opened them. I picked out a black tapestry pencil skirt, glossy black tights, tall black and cream Manolos a cream Dior silk shirt with a black diamanté collar. I asked for the hairdresser to be sent up and it a few moments my dark hair was glossy and coiffured in an up-do, matt red lipstick, black eye-liner over gold powder eye shadow completed the look. I stared at myself in the mirror. Perfect. Same but different.

Later in the day I booked myself into the famous Spa for a facial and a massage, and by the evening I was starving for a steak medium rare and a salad with a glass of champagne, hopefully to wake up in the morning without finding a yet another star shaped corpse in the front garden.

I had my meal served in my room and waited for a knock on the front door.

It was about 11.30pm when Toby arrived.

"All right missus? " he asked as I opened the door to him. It was as if he saw me glammed up everyday of the week.

"How are my babies?" I asked handing him a glass of champagne.

"Fine, fed, watered, walked, fussed."he took the glass and swigged it in one go.

He sat in the mock French 17th century armchair.

"James Constable didn't seem too upset about his father's wife." I said to him.

"To him she was just his father's wife, even though she was James' stepmother and she'd been his stepmother since he was twelve."

Toby got up and poured some water into the kettle and turned it on. "He'd always hated her from the day she married his father. But not enough to kill her, especially now, I heard down the pub he was up for promotion." He put a tea bag into a cup and poured hot water on it. "Want one?"

"I'll stick with this." I sipped my Bollinger, "Bet that won't happen now."

"I dunno about that, he always was a jammy bugger, the sort of lad who'd fall in a pile of manure and come up smelling of roses with a twenty pound note in his hand." he sipped his tea.

I laughed, I knew the type only too well. "Why my house? It's like I've got a gianormous murderous cat bringing me gifts and leaving them on the doorstep."

It was his turn to laugh and he spluttered his tea. "Couple of years ago anything could have been dumped up there and no-one would have noticed, the front was so overgrown you wouldn't have known there was a house there at all. It was only when Dirty Dawkins' brother turned up to claim his inheritance that the house was cleared up a bit."

"Dirty Dawkins?" I asked bemused.

He laughed out loud, "Ever since I was a kid he was a filthy old sod. Piles of rubbish everywhere, never washed anything, not even himself. He hung stuff out on the line – not washed - just to air, when the smell got too bad even for him."

I shuddered. "Revolting – bleugh!"

"Strange thing was he was always polite and kind. Smelly he might have been, but my mother always said he had the manners of a gentleman."

He sipped his tea again. "But..."

"But?" I asked watching a smile crinkle the corners of his lips.

"On Sundays, over the top of his work clothes, he worked at Sunnyhill farm as a labourer, he would put on a flowery dress and an old straw hat with a red ribbon and cycle down to the church for the sermon. Regular as clockwork."

I laughed, "Probably the only clean clothes he had."

"By the way, James' stepmum and his dad were separated, rumour in the village was that she was having an affair." he plonked back into the armchair.

"Join the WI missus, they have all the gossip, but watch em, my mum says if you get involved with that lot if they're not talking about someone else, they'll be talking about you!"

When he left about 1am I put on a cream silk nightdress, picked up one of a pile of murder mysteries I'd bought in Waterstones earlier that day and read it in the hope of getting some clue to what was happening.

I was woken by the sun streaming through the shutters, I looked at the bedside clock 8.30am. If I hurried I could still make breakfast. I walked over and peered out of the newly painted white shutters onto the square below. Leaves were starting to fall covering the circle of tired grass with orange and gold hues. The soft pale Bath stone was being lit yellow by the early morning sun.

I took a sharp breath, a bright red Mercedes like the one that had almost clipped my car yesterday was parked under a tree on the opposite side of the road outside another elegant Georgian hotel.

Trying not to feel rattled, I showered and dressed and ate my breakfast of crispy bacon, mushrooms, tomatoes and toast at the table by the window, watching the car.

A dark haired woman, elegant, middle fifties, with an upswept hairdo, and a scarf tied around her neck in the latest fashion was talking to a grey haired tanned man. He put his arm around her waist. They were obviously a couple, little touches, little kisses.

She was wearing expensive jeans and a blue and white striped designer shirt. I smiled, although I didn't recognise them from Overdown, I felt this was an illicit affair. She got into her red Mercedes waved kisses at him and drove off.

So the near collision yesterday was co-incidence. Bath is only an hour or so from Overdown, perhaps she was driving through to get here yesterday. She was going in the right direction.

Feeling slightly happier, I went shopping at Debenhams and then M&S to buy some smart drab clothes for Hilary to wear to the WI. Then after lunch at Pret, I drove through the afternoon sunshine back to Overdown, hoping that I wouldn't find another body of a local dignitary on my front lawn.

When I arrived home, I was surprised to find that the lawn had been cut and the hedges were a good half a metre shorter, the front of the house had been jet washed, and the Cotswold stone at last showed it's true colour.

Toby was in the kitchen cutting himself a doorstep of bread and plonking a lump of cheese on it.

"Hello Missus" he grinned spitting crumbs at me.

"Thank you, the house looks wonderful, you've done so much." I had dropped my case in the hall and now had my hands around the tea pot, it was hot.

"Just made a pot" he took a cup from the rack and poured me some."nice break?"

"Yes lovely, - why did you do all this?" I asked sipping the sweet black tea.

"Well, I had the animals at mine, and this do make a lot of noise. I thought I'd get it done and bring them back when I'd finished." He took a bite of doorstep and cheese, "I'll fetch em over this afternoon."

He picked up his tea and had a gulp, "Oh by the way, the cops want to see you again."

"Why? " I asked despondently.

"Dunno, they just said you have to pop into the station when you get back." he said.

"So they came over, and said you were allowed to clear up the front garden?" I asked suddenly craving a chocolate biscuit.

"Yes, they said they had all they needed, and they took your gun." He put his cup in the top of the dishwasher.

Suddenly life had become surreal again. "Gun?" I asked surprised, "I don't have a gun. Never had a gun." I ripped open the biscuit barrel and stuffed a jammie dodger and a double choc chip into my mouth and swallowed like a gannet.

"It's all right, it wasn't the gun that killed the Chief Constable." he smiled.

"But I don't have a gun." I finished my hot tea, "I'm going into Overdown see you later."

"Hold on Missus can you pay my invoice before you go?" he pushed it across to me on the kitchen worktop. I read the invoice, took out my cheque book and wrote out a cheque for twice the amount he'd charged me. "Can you start on the back now? Repair and paint the sheds, clear the back of the garden, get rid of all those old elder tree and convolvulous.

"What?" He picked up the cheque.

"Columbine." I answered starting to head for the door.

"I know what columbine is." he answered."But this is too much." he waved my cheque at me.

"No it isn't," I shouted from my car, "I'll talk to you about it later."

Toby stood in my doorway cheque in one hand and cup of tea in the other looking confused.

"Don't get killed." I shouted at him as I drove off.

"Not planning on it." he shouted back waving the cheque.

Overdown was a quaint little village with lots of honey coloured Jacobean houses with a few tall Georgian ones sprinkled in between for good measure. The ancient buttercross stood on a roundabout in the middle of the village and a farmers market had been held there on Thursdays since medieval times. Butchers,bakers,antique shops and estate agents filled the high street, at the back of which, overlooking the Manor grounds and the river were a couple of old English tea shops, and the Manor shop.

The church stood tall and Norman at the top of the hill behind the Buttercross and the Tourist Information was on the corner by the Herbal Tea Shop.

I didn't know where the Police station was so I went into the Tourist Information to ask.

A tubby girl in a navy uniform with a face like a scrubbed pork pie came up to me.

"Can I help you?" she asked in a flat monotone staring at my new jumper.

"Can you tell me where the police station is?" I asked.

"Who wants to know?" she asked flatly.

"Stacey." I woman's voice came from the office behind the counter. "We've talked about this."

"What?" Stacey looked offended.

"Go and make some tea, I'll deal with this." A middle aged woman with short grey hair came round the corner from the office.

"Sorry about that, she's a trainee."

I nearly made a wisecrack but bit my tongue as she looked like a really nice woman. She took a map out. "The police station is in the Buttercross, upstairs – is it urgent? Because they won't be there until 2.00 tomorrow."

"Oh." I must have looked surprised.

"There's only two of them and they're out in the patrol car at the moment." she smiled at me.

I held out my hand for her to shake. "I'm Hilary Long from Coldcross Cottage, and I really must change that name."

"Oh you poor dear." She called to her assistant, "Stacey make another tea please."

A drone came from the back office "Do I have to?"

"Yes you do." she said, as she led me to the back window of the shop with two modern leather square shaped sofas and a coffee table, there was a view of the church, the Manor house and the road towards Tewkesbury.

"I'm Marjorie Crawley." she said sitting down.

The scrubbed pork pie with the scraped back dirty blonde ponytail brought us two teas and some custard creams on a saucer. She put them down and stood like a monolith over us.

"Can you man the front desk Stacey?" asked Marjorie, "We've got some visitors." She nodded to two young backpackers routing through the leaflets of places to go.

"If I have to." Stacey said in her usual monotone and slommacked off to intimidate the visitors.

"I just want to say this sort of thing has never happened before in this village so please don't be put off." She passed me a tea.

"Well I didn't know either of the people very well, or at all really. I looked down the pretty street. "But I came here for peace and quiet and if anything it's been worse than living in London." I picked up my tea and sipped it.

"Oh, I am sorry." Marjorie sipped her tea, "It's been a big blow to the community here, the Reverend Hart was a very dynamic vicar, his church has a big congregation and they'll be lost without him." She smiled, "some of the old ladies will miss him especially."

"Do you know his wife? Do you think I should visit her?" As I put my cup down I realised my hand was shaking.

Marjorie put her hand over mine."Go and see the Doctor."

"I don't want tranquillisers." I said, my voice wobbly.

"No, I understand, try Angela next door, get some camomile tea."

"I don't know what to do now, they said they needed to see me today."

I got up to go.

Marjorie picked up some glossy books from a shelf near to where she was sitting. "They'll be in the Red Lion about 8.00, they go there after work for their dinner and a pint. Here take these." She pushed a couple of the glossy books on Overdown into my hand. "Pay me when you're next in the village."

As I stood up to leave I heard Stacey animated for the first time since I walked into the shop.

"You go see Overdown man right? He's really cool right, and the old castle." she shut up immediately I came into view. "All right?" she droned.

"Thanks," I smiled, I turned to Marjorie,"Overdown man?"

She grinned broadly showing pink lipstick on her teeth which I forgave her for as she was so nice. "On the road down there, left and left again."

"Like Piltdown Man?" I asked.

"More modern." she grinned.

I walked down the road to my car, got in and thought I'd take a look.

I took the Tewkesbury road and turned left down a narrow lane, and left again, as I turned the corner I saw a crumbling ruined castle on top of the hill, and on the side of the hill facing the road was a giant figure cut out of the chalk. A Piltdown man, the same shape and size but wearing a beanie and instead of a club he was giving the world a finger.

I almost wet myself laughing! So Overdown does have a fun side.

I drove back to the cottage smiling and feeling calmer, Toby was packing up his van.

"Finished already?" I asked.

"Got to go home sometime." he grinned.

"Thanks for everything." I opened the door to see Miss Marple and Poirot side by side, heads in their dinner dishes.

I didn't feel like going out again, the front lawn looked good, a microwave dinner was calling to my stomach and I could barely keep my eyes open. I poured myself a nice cold cranberry juice, pinged my dinner and sat and ate in front of the TV. My reasoning being if I don't sit at the table in the window then another resident of Overdown will not end up on my front lawn in the middle of the night.

Poirot started to bark and scratch at the front door. It was the reason I got him, but as I had a mouthful of lasagne it was just a bit inconvenient.

I opened the door and a very elderly lady was sprinkling red roses on my front lawn.

"What the fuck are you doing on my property?" I shouted holding Poirot back by his collar.

"I'm paying my respects to Reverend Hart." She gave me a glassy hard stare

"I wouldn't expect you to understand you didn't know him."

"Get out of my garden." I shouted at her.

"You've been here five minutes, I've been here seventy years." she stood upright stick in hand."I'm not going anywhere."

"Don't you think I've had enough people in my front garden in the last two days?" Poirot was choking on his collar so I pushed him inside.

"All right if you insist." she said walking towards the door.

I stood in her way. "Insist on what?"

"Me leaving the garden." she pushed past me opened my door and walked in.

"What are you doing?" I asked as she sat at the table near the window and looked at the mess of red roses on my newly mown and previously neat front lawn.

"Paying my respects, I told you." she stared round the room. "You've worked very hard here, this place was a pigsty." She picked up Miss Marple and put her on her lap. "White, no sugar." she gave me that glassy look again, "You do know how to make tea I suppose?"

I kept an eye on her from the kitchen, two things I did know - one, she definitely wasn't a vampire as she had come in uninvited and the second was that despite her age she was not frightened of anything. She stared at the mess on my lawn till dusk fell silently sipping her tea. Then as the street lights came on in Underdown she got up stiffly, straightened up letting my kitten fall to the floor and walked to the door.

"Thank you." she said without emotion,

"Do you want a lift into the village?" I asked trying to make sure she would go.

"I don't live in the village, I live near the bottom of the hill." she stared at me. "My car is outside."

"You drive?" I asked surprised.

"Well, I didn't push it up here." she said shortly.

I watched as her little white fiat panda rolled off down the hill. I closed the door and put the latch across. At least she's not dead on my lawn.

I was almost scared to look out of the top window the following morning and put off the moment by opening a few boxes and unpacking them. When I did look all I saw were a dozen red roses and black clouds rolling over the hills bringing rain towards me. I raced out, picked up the roses quickly and put them in the garden waste bin.

It was Saturday already, all the days had rolled into one last week, it had gone so fast. Not the sort of week I'd want anyone to have.

I fed Miss Marple, picking her up and putting her on the worktop. Her tiny tabby face looked so sweet with a bit of cat meat stuck to the tip of her little pink nose. "Hello sweetheart." I stroked her soft fur and she shivered with delight, purring and eating. I kissed the top of her tiny silver and black head. Poirot was bouncing about wanting attention, so I fed him in his metal dish on the floor. I had tried feeding them together but Poirot ate Miss Marple's dinner and his own in two seconds flat.

Miss Marple walked across the kitchen sink and looked out of the window into the garden, within seconds she was asleep on the windowsill. I washed the worktops, washed their dishes, and washed the chair and table where the old lady had been sitting last night.

I thundered upstairs dragged on some trakkie bottoms a bra and tee shirt and went to the door. "Out?" I asked the bouncing Poirot. "Going out?" he seemed to grin as I attached his lead and in no time at all he was dragging me along the top lane.

I hadn't realised that after her separation Chief Constable Christine West had rented a cottage about four hundred yards from my own. Constable Constable was standing outside with a tall sandy haired man, very upright, with greying sideburns and a touch of grey above his forehead. The wind on the hill was whipping their words towards me, I slowed down, Poirot was doing his business, so I had a chance to listen.

"Who would do this James?" The older man asked.

"She was Chief Constable, father." Constable Constable answered, "It could have been anyone."

"Have forensics any idea of the shotgun used?" the older man asked.

"Yes, but there are loads of them down here, every farmer owns that sort of shotgun." James replied.

"Can it be matched to any particular gun?" his father asked.

"Possibly, but that would mean collecting every gun in the area." James sighed, "There's only me and Darren and Trevor, he issues the gun licences.

I think I can get another officer from Underdown on overtime."

"Well do it," his father stared at him, "Get off your arse boy and get more professional, do you want to be stuck in this backwater forever?"

I could hear James shuffle uncomfortably.

I was putting poo in a plastic bag when Constable Constable walked past.

"No more bodies on your lawn this morning?" he asked sarcastically.

"Are you going to introduce us?" asked his father.

"Hilary Long." James said with an edge in his voice. "My father, Colonel Charles Constable."

The Colonel offered his hand.

"Sorry Colonel, I've just been cleaning up after my dog, so I won't shake hands."

He put his hand in his pocket."So, you've got old Dirty's place eh?"

I could see him weighing me up trying to read me.

"I'm sorry for your loss." I said pulling Poirot to heel.

"Well, Well," he said gruffly, "Funeral's on Friday week, you should come, as I hear you were such good friends with Christine."He started to walk off down the lane to his Landrover, he turned, "12.00 Overdown Church wear black."

"Why wouldn't I wear black?" I asked aloud.

"If it wasn't for you she wouldn't be dead." James snarled at me.

"You can't say that." I retorted, "If you had been doing your job you would have had some sort of clue by now."

"About your gun," he said changing the subject.

"I don't have a gun." I stared at him.

"We searched your house," he smiled insolently, "We found it hidden up the chimney."

"I didn't see a warrant." I answered annoyed.

"Mr Thicko was there, he had to let us in."

"You're looking in the wrong place." I pulled Poirot away from Constable Constable's leg, he was eyeing it suspiciously, probably going to shag it or pee on it.

"Where's Christine's car?" I asked, "Where did she go after she left me?"

"Home I suppose." he flushed red.

"What was Reverend Hart doing on this hill in the middle of the night? Could it have been Christine?"

"Don't say that." James snapped at me, he obviously felt more for his stepmother than he realised.

"Come to the station and pick up your gun so that I can arrest you for being in possession without a licence." he grinned broadly, "Unless," he leered.

"In your dreams Constable Constable. I'll be there at 11.30." I let Poirot pee on his leg and we both jogged off back towards my cottage leaving James standing in a puddle of green water.

After a strong cup of coffee, a shower, and putting on some jeans and a jumper, I phoned Toby to ask about the search and the gun.

"I forgot, I was so busy, sorry missus, I followed them round and made sure they didn't wreck anything."

"The gun, where did they find the gun?" I asked impatiently.

"Up the chimney on a ledge. It's very old covered in soot and muck."

"But I had that chimney cleaned." I said surprised.

"I suppose it got missed as it was on a ledge tucked away, they found a shoe as well." He laughed, "my mum was right interested, she's well into history.

You met her the other day, she works at the Tourist Information in town."

When I put the phone down on Toby I picked it up again to ring a number he'd given me.

Bang on 11.30 Marjorie Crawley and I walked up the stairs in the ancient buttercross to the police station. It seemed very secure with the desk behind some strengthened glass, Marjorie pressed the button and called through the speaker panel.

"Darren, James." and we waited hearing rustling from the room beyond.

"Hello," PC Lowndes smiled at me, "Hello Marjorie."

"I've come about the gun," I smiled what I thought was sweetly, but was probably through gritted teeth because Darren looked quite scared as he rushed off to get it.

"It's about 1625, a musket." Marjorie smiled surprised. As she saw Darren walking through to the interview room carrying it. He opened the door for us.

"Wow, that's very accurate." I smiled amazed.

"It's the shoe tied to the stock that gives it away. If I can have it for the museum I can date it properly." Marjorie reached out to touch it, wanting to have a really good look, but Constable Constable shouted from the back office. "Where's your licence?" He walked round the corner and leant on the desk smiling smugly.

"It's decommissioned," Marjorie smiled. "There's no trigger mechanism. Anyway it's an archaeological find. Get Trevor over to decommission it properly." She turned to me, "Then can I have it for the museum?"

"Of course." I smiled, Marjorie was a gem like her son.

"Trevor's here." smiled PC Lowndes."Helping us out with Christine's murder."

"Trevor." Marjorie called with a smile on her lips, "How are you me old duck?"

Marjorie seemed to know everyone.

A stocky bald policeman came over and joined the discussion. "Hello old love." he grinned at her, "after the musket for the museum?"

"And the shoe." she smiled.

"Can I sign it over? Do I have to do something like that?" I asked.

Constable Constable lost interest and walked over to a huge pile of shotguns and rifles on a table in the back room. Some in covers and some without.

"I'll sort it." smiled Trevor, "I could do with a nice easy job."

He came back with some papers and put them on the table. He gestured to the armoury on the back wall, "Now that, is a hell of a job, I've had to confiscate every firearm in the village and I've still got to go up to the manor to get theirs." He pushed the forms towards me "Sign there." I signed them and then Marjorie signed them.

"All yours now me duck." Trevor smiled at Marjorie. "I'll bring it to the museum tomorrow about 11.00 after I've been to the manor."

"Thanks Trevor, and don't forget the shoe." Marjorie seemed really pleased to be able to get her hands on a bit of history.

Well, I think that's what it was.

"Time for a coffee?" I asked Marjorie.

"Lovely." she smiled. "I hear my Toby's doing great at your place."

We walked across the road to the coffee shop and managed to get a window seat.

"Yes he is." I picked up the menu, I could eat what I liked now, well, within reason. "He's a really good worker."

"Took the business over from his dad, promised to keep the business running and he has." She picked up the menu I'd just put down.

"Sorry," I said assuming that Marjorie was a widow.

"God no, he's not dead." she laughed a little too loudly and avoided my eyes, concentrating on the menu. "He's working on rigs off Scotland."

"Making money." I smiled.

"Enough for us to retire to Spain in two years. Can't wait.

"Toby?" I asked, "Going with?"

"No." she smiled, "He's happy here."

I ordered a skinny latte and a cappuccino and two chocolate wafer biscuits.

I wondered why Toby was happy here. I wondered if I could ever be happy here. I thought about my Cadogan Square flat, and my flat in the Docklands, I told my friends I was selling them because the areas were so passé now. It bought me the cottage with tons to spare.

The coffees arrived and Marjorie stared at me as she took hers.

"What is it?"

"What is what?" I asked, this woman was bright.

"Come now, you want to ask me something." she sipped her cappuccino leaving a white moustache on her upper lip, which I again forgave her for because she was becoming a friend.

"An old lady, a strange old lady, elegant, upright – and very brusque came and threw a dozen red roses on my front lawn, pushed her way into my cottage, drank my tea and stared at the lawn until dusk, paying her respects she tells me and then drives off in a little blue Fiat Panda."

"Aah," Marjorie sighed, as she bit a piece of biscuit. "That was dear old Mrs Walker, she was at one time, many years ago quite a famous ballerina – Royal Ballet I think it was –

had the world at her feet. Met and married Alastair Walker, the writer, they had no children, but it was said he was a jealous man, controlling, and Alice was very beautiful."

"So she was widowed? When?" I asked.

"About a week after the Reverend Hart joined the Parish, he conducted the funeral. He was a great support to her,"

"How long ago was that?" I asked sipping my latte, staring at the drops of summer rain falling big and splashy, onto the baked dry pavements.

"Oh, twenty years or so now." She stared into the street, "I suppose Autumn is on the way now."

"A murderer always returns to the scene of the crime," I said bluntly, "that's what all the books say."

"Mrs Walker?" she asked, but I could see her mind was working on the thought.

"Why not?" I watched her face, "He was up visiting Christine West – but where had he been before that?"

Without thinking too much, I could see Marjorie was putting two and two together, but worried it might come to five, said nothing.

"You know something." I sipped my coffee.

"Maybe nothing." She cradled her cup in her hands, "But he did have dinner with her every Thursday evening for the past twenty years. Started off as a comfort thing as she'd just lost her husband, and his wife was pleased, gave her a night off to go into town, see a show and have a few cocktails with her friends. It meant nothing to either of them."

"It meant everything to Mrs Walker." The words came out before the thoughts had even crossed my mind.

"You have to leave." I smiled at the figure in my bed, his hair was tousled and he smiled back at me.

"Why?"

"Because my gardener is coming at 11.00." I walked into the shower after a very satisfying and unexpected evening of passionate love making.

He walked into the shower with me, lifted my hair and kissed the back of my neck. I turned and stroked his wet hair off his face and kissed him. "No more, not now." I smiled as I slipped out of the shower and wrapped myself in a towel. Popped my dressing gown over the top and went downstairs to feed my pets.

At 11.00 exactly Toby was at the door.

"Morning missus." he grinned broadly.

"Mrs Walker, where does she live?" I asked jogging past in my trakkies with Poirot bouncing along beside me."

"Next to Christine West, well two cottages along." he pulled a heavy toolbox into the hall.

"Are you sure you can fix the tiles on the roof and those loose floorboards?"

"Handyman/Gardener." he pointed to the side of his van. "Look that's what it says."

"Okay, I'm going to see Mrs Walker. Don't get killed." I jogged out of the garden with Poirot in hot pursuit.

"Try not to." he laughed.

Alice Walker's cottage was not easy to find, yes there were only two cottages in the road, but there were others tucked behind them, and I had forgotten how rampant sex makes you feel the following day. Fantastic, yes, but my jogging was wobbly. I remembered where I saw Constable Constable and his father and counted two doors up from the cottage sideways on and set back from the road.

Alice was in the garden, she'd picked up her milk from the step and was dead heading the red roses by her gate.

I walked past her into her house and sat at her table she stared at me then a smile crept across her lips.

"Tea?" she asked heading for the kitchen.

"Not from you." I answered shortly, "Why did you do it?" Poirot was snuffling about so I picked him up and after wriggling for a bit he decided to be good and sat on my lap and looked out of the window.

"Do what?" she smiled a smile that would curdle milk, as she poured hot water onto a teabag in a cup for herself.

I took a breath, should I come straight out with it or beat about the bush?

"Kill Reverend Hart."

Her hand didn't even shake as she sat down. "Oh my dear, fancy yourself as a detective do you?" She sipped her black tea, over her shoulder on the sideboard was a framed photograph of her with Margot Fonteyn dressed as chorus swans from Swan Lake, they were both very young and beautiful.

"What if I did ? Who would believe you?"

I stared at her clutching Poirot so hard he squeaked.

"I loved him, Richard was my heart, my soul-mate from the moment I met him," she sipped her tea again her thin lips reddening with the heat from the cup. "Intelligent, handsome, together we had the perfect love, not the sort of filthy game you seem to indulge in."

I pushed my glasses up my nose, this old lady was frightening me, something in her had changed and her face became cold and hard.

"We didn't need sex, life isn't all about sex." she hissed.

"Do you regret it? " I asked holding tight to the wriggling Poirot. "Not having sex with your husband or your soul-mate?"

"Clever girl." she smiled icily."No, I didn't want children, I wanted to stay slim and dance forever."

"So when your husband started having affairs, you poisoned him and Richard Hart came into your life."I stroked Poirot in the hope he'd stay still.

"No, no, no, I thought you'd got it. I poisoned my husband because I fell in love with Richard, and it was a way of getting him to be with me, to comfort me." She picked up a photo of a white haired elegant handsome man and stroked a bony finger across it. "Alastair was gay, as you call it now, and we were happy in our way, he was always worried someone would steal me away when we were younger and he'd be found out and disinherited. But I stayed, I didn't have to have sex so it suited us both." She put the photo back on the mantelpiece. "We were both respectable,he was the son of a Lord you know." She stared across at me with cold blue eyes. "I assume you have tape recorded this."

I said nothing but the voice record on my android phone was on in my pocket.

"He was going to leave his wife for that stupid woman next door, it would have been the end of his career, he would have had to move away with her, and I would never see him again." She smiled putting her cup in the sink, "Well, I couldn't have that, could I ? Now he'll be in Overdown forever and I can go and talk to him as I used to."

"You are an awful person." I couldn't help myself saying."You lied to me saying you lived at the bottom of the hill. "

"Yes, but I was more beautiful than you are, more famous, more loved." She touched her toes easily as if to prove a point. "More limber."

If only you knew, I thought to myself with a little secret smile.

She stood upright and I lifted Poirot under my arm and stood and faced her.

"How did he end up in my garden ?" I asked trying to distract her so I could get away.

"Well, the ground glass was taking so long, I had to hurry things up. I'd been giving him little doses of arsenic every time he came, in tea, in his food. The glass was in ice cream or sorbet," she smiled to herself, "he loved my sorbet. Poor man he thought he was getting an ulcer, used to have stomach bleeds you know, and men." She stared at me with her glassy blue eyes. "Hate going to see the doctor."

She templed her fingers to her lips. "I heard them arguing in the lane, they were so loud. So I went and stood by the gate and asked him in."

She tried to stroke Poirot's forehead but he snarled at her.

"Anyway, I asked him in for a drink, to calm him down, he wouldn't say what they were arguing about." her voice became bitter. "But I knew, it was about leaving his wife, his church, his village. So a double whiskey and soda became a rather strong mix of something else. He'd parked his car at the bottom of the lane, and I followed him saying I 'd walk up as far as your house and then go home. After I left him I think he realised something was very wrong, saw your light on and tried to go for help."

She stifled a giggle." Funny really I turned round to see him trip on that large stone with the boot scraper by your gate and he just went flying into the air and landed in your garden." She laughed, "You had to see it to believe it!"

Her face suddenly changed, "No-one will believe you my dear, and I can't see a recording device on your skimpy clothes, not unless it's in your little doggie." She put her face close to Poirot's and he snarled and barked at her.

"You have something to hide, don't you dear?" she smiled.

"Keep away from me." I gave her a Paddington hard stare, "and my house."

She walked to the door and opened it. "Can't promise," she smirked, "I rather like your house, I see you threw my roses away. I might have to plant a rose bush as a house-warming gift. Then I can come and visit."

She closed the door after me and I could hear her laughing.

Anger burnt through me, I could feel my blood boiling, I jogged down the road not looking where I was going and barrelled straight into Colonel Constable's chest.

"You all right?" he asked. "Glad you ran into me, would you go through Christine's papers with me on Wednesday as you were a friend of hers?"

"Yes." I said without thinking, "Can you come back to my cottage and I'll make a list of what you want me to do."

"Certainly, I was headed there anyway to ask you if you'd help."

I watched Alice's smirking face from behind the hedge as the Colonel, Poirot and me walked the short distance to my cottage.

"Come in." I said urgently. I opened the garden door, "Toby come here please." he dropped his tools and obeyed immediately.

"We don't need your gardener for this do we?" the Colonel asked bemused as he sat on my shabby chic sofa and Toby stood in the doorway to the kitchen.

I took my phone out of my pocket, put it in the docking cradle and soon Alice's' acid tones filled my lovely home, the ancient poison of her words, cold and precise echoed through the silence of Dirty Dawkins cottage.

"My God." The Colonel stood up with a start and pulled out his mobile phone. Toby stared at me I knew he believed me unquestioningly as the evil cold voice poisoned the atmosphere around us.

I will really have to move after this I thought, I have by accident solved a murder in my own back yard, well two if you count Alice's husband.

The Colonel didn't call Constable Constable or Constable Lowndes, he called his wife's old number and spoke to the new chief who was also a good friend of his.

Quietly and without fuss, Alice disappeared overnight into custody, almost by stealth she was gone and strangely so was my android phone. There would be no more red roses in my garden, scattered or otherwise, and no grieving parishioner at Richard Hart's grave, who would no doubt smother it with red rose petals.

Later that evening I was trying to drink myself into oblivion, and had just got through my second bottle of red. My thinking being – white is less in calories, but red is good for your heart. Poirot started barking at the front door. I opened it wearing Miss Marple as a shawl.

"Colonel Constabble." I slurred, "what can I do for you?" I burped and a mouthful of red wine acid and cheese on toast popped out of my stomach.

I swallowed it down. "Sorry."

"Drinking eh?" he asked brusquely. "Got any Scotch?"

"Yes." I gestured to the living room and Miss Marple slid down my arm with the kind of grace that no cat could have planned, onto the back of the sofa, landing on the sofa but leaving me with red track marks on my skin.

"Scotch or Irish?" I shouted from the kitchen.

"Scotch." he shouted back.

I poured almost half a pint of Scotch into a glass and threw in a handful of ice and came back with yet another red wine in my glass.

"I say, how did you know I liked ice in my Scotch?" he asked.

"I didn't" I covered a burp with my hand, "Just I do."

We sat drinking in silence, Poirot sat between us eyeing the Colonel suspiciously.

Eventually the Colonel spoke.

"Rum old do this." he said sipping his drink.

"Your son is a twat." I slurred.

The Colonel garrumphed as only a Colonel can. "We think he was switched at the hospital, anyway watch your language young lady."

"I know a lot of language." I slurred, "I worked in a Library."

"Inner London?" he asked.

I garrumphed as only a lying runaway millionairess can.

"What will happen to her ?" I asked strangely sober.

"She'll be committed, she's far too old to go to prison, she'll spend the rest of her days in a secure asylum we think."

"Good." I felt really sick now and as I didn't want to throw up on another constable I walked him to the door.

"Wednesday." he said shortly. Drinking down his scotch in one go.

"Wednesday." I answered impressed.

I could hear his shoes crunch on my path as I threw up in the Butler sink I loved so much.

I woke up with a thick headache and could hardly bend down to feed Poirot and Miss Marple. It felt like a ton of bricks had fallen forward into the front of my head. I stood up and ran water into the sink watching the diced carrot whirl into the macerator. I almost made more join it.

I stood in the shower for ages, the hot needles of water forcing me back to humanity. I dried off put on my dressing gown and made myself a strong black coffee and a bacon bagel. I took one bite of it and started to cry thinking of my docklands flat and him, he who made me bacon bagels every weekend. He'd climb back into bed and we'd laugh and chat and read the papers in bed.

Now he thought I was dead. How could I do that to him?

I ate my bagel and drank my coffee with tears running down my face. It was the Reverend Hart's funeral today but that wasn't why I was crying.

I pulled out a sober grey and black suit and a grey shirt, sensible shoes and a handbag. I stood in front of the mirror and put on my Hilary Long make up. Light foundation a bit of mascara and a pink lipstick that didn't suit me. I got into my car and drove into Overdown to the church.

Where was Christine's car? I suddenly thought, she came to see me on the way home from work, drove to me, and yet her car wasn't outside her house or mine, and it wasn't in a ditch or the police would have found it. Even the local Laurel and Hardy police couldn't have missed a pale blue BMW in a hedge.

I drove down to the church parked up and walked in, I sat beside Marjorie as I knew no-one else. The coffin came in carried by Reverend Hart's son and three pall bearers, they put the coffin on the stand near the Altar and bowed their heads respectfully.

The Bishop of Gloucester took the service, marking how important the Reverend Hart was to the church. The Norman church was full and hushed as Reverend Hart's favourite hymn was played and the choir sang.

Lady Dorcas Fellowes Hart and her daughter a pretty fair haired debutante called Cecilia sat in the front pew, and soon John, the son, joined them. He was tall with curly fair hair and quite chinless, but the aristocracy always have a confident air, even when completely clueless, as he appeared to be.

I thought that in the right light if you were completely pissed, he might even seem handsome.

As I listened to the Bishop expound the qualities of the Reverend Hart DSO and Bar my head was pounding so loudly I thought everyone could hear it.

I pulled my glasses off for a second and rubbed my eyes with my fingertips.

"Are you all right?" Marjorie whispered.

"Just tired and emotional." I whispered back truthfully.

I felt another pair of eyes on the back of my neck, but I didn't turn round, I knew who it was.

Lady Dorcas Fellowes Hart got up to speak, she didn't go to the lectern but stood beside her husband's coffin and rested her long elegant fingers on the edge of it.

"Richard, my darling husband always knew what I wanted and always went out of his way to get it for me. Whatever it was." She took a breath and looked across to her son and daughter in the front pews and it was at that moment that I recognised where I'd seen her before.

She had a black and gold print scarf carefully draped over her designer black suit, her fair hair coiffured, fluffy, now white in places. She wore dark blue eyeshadow as if she's crushed a child's crumbly crayon over each eye. An artificial tear ran down her cheek.

"He was a good husband, father, friend and Vicar, and he didn't deserve this to happen to him, he deserved to be happy for the rest of his life, and that didn't happen for him."

There was a hushed murmur from the congregation.

"Goodbye Richard, happy yomping darling." She walked away from the coffin with the green beret on and sat emotionless in the pew.

After the burial I found myself standing in the Manor for the first time. I felt uncomfortable being there, as if I didn't belong, amongst these people who had known each other for years. They had grown up together, gone to school together, lived together.

Not my tribe, I was an incomer. But there was something else, someone else. I walked to the stone Jacobean fireplace and stood looking at the flowers standing in the grate.

"Sorcha?" I heard a familiar voice, but I didn't turn round. Like Superman I hid behind my big black Kent glasses and Majorie came over with a sherry for me. "Thank you." I smiled at her

He caught my arm, so I had to look at him with my brown clear glass contact lenses. "Sorcha?"

Majorie had walked to the table to get a sandwich and talk to her friends but came back when she saw I was uncomfortable with my "new" acquaintance. I gave her what I thought was a distressed look.

"Hilary." she smiled, "Come and meet Laura." she took me by the elbow and pulled me over to the sandwiches.

"Excuse me." I said as I bustled past him and stood together backs to him as I met Laura, head of the local WI, and probably the most boring woman on the planet. When Laura moved on to socialise I spoke to Marjorie.

"Who is he?" I asked as if I didn't know.

"Armand du Champ, an old friend of the family, he's a city banker." She smiled at me. "Well?"

"Well what?" I asked munching a ham sandwich.

"If he fancies you, you'll be set for life." she grinned wickedly,"Look he's coming over."

"Where's the loo?" I asked dropping my sandwich. "I don't like the look of him he's leery.",

"Just by the front door on the left." Majorie smiled as I rushed off in the direction of the loo, leaving Armand to talk to Majorie.

I went past the lavatory and out of the front door looking for somewhere to hide, my heart was pounding so loudly I was sure they could hear it.

I ran out of the Portico and the shuttered front windows, to the back of the house. There was a magnificent view of the castle ruins, some battered and broken sheds adjoining some empty dilapidated stables, I went through one of the stable doors, the back of the stables were non existant where time had taken it's toll.

I could see the front of the house through a crack in the stable door, I knew Armand of old, he wouldn't stay long, just long enough to pay his respects and to look the part of an old friend. But his real friend was money, and he would not leave it alone for long, and when the call of the city beckoned he would be gone.

I looked round in the dusty half-light and caught a glimpse of something blue, just a shiny reflection where the sun was creeping through the broken wooden slats of the wall. I was going to investigate when I heard the low throaty roar of Armand's Ferrari and saw it disappear up the drive and through the gates of the Manor into one-way system of Overdown's tiny town centre.

I went back into the Manor, Marjorie was now standing with her son, who suited and booted looked quite different from his normal shabby self.

"What did he want?" I asked speaking to Marjorie and ignoring Toby who was smiling at me.

"He thought he knew you, and was very interested in you until I told you you were my cousin from Milton Keynes, and that you worked in a library there and you came back home for the funeral." She smiled.

Marjorie seemed an accomplished liar, but I was grateful.

"He said you have a double in London."

"That creeps me out." I shuddered, "But what if he checks your story?"

Toby grinned. "Facebook, we found another Hilary Long – librarian like you – no photo, but does work in Milton Keynes. So we borrowed her identity."

"Thank you," I smiled, "Thank you so much." I didn't explain, there would be time for that later.

The mourners were leaving, I watched the various groups, the WI, the Churchwomen's guild, nattering about Alice, worried they hadn't seen her for days.

Old Army buddies, old school friends of whom Armand had been one. Shaking Lady Dorca's hand, smiling sadly, the younger mourners hugged Cecilia and John, the elegant pastel blue and white morning room full of exquisite 18th century French furniture was emptying. Soon it was my turn.

"Thank you for inviting me, it must have been strange for you." I smiled at the ageing beauty.

"Well," she whispered, "You found his murderer, he was in your garden, I thought it might bring you closure."

"I'm sorry I couldn't help him, that I didn't realise he was there. I felt awful that he came to me for help and I didn't even realise."

It was true, and something I had thought long and hard about, and was one of the reasons I thought about leaving Overdown.

Dorcas smiled, "You found his killer, I'm sure he'll forgive you, he was that sort of man." She took a breath, "Armand thought he knew you."

"Who?" I faked looking puzzled. "Was that the tall man with the greying hair who came over to me? I wondered what that was about, he made me feel very uncomfortable, I had to leave." I realised I was talking too much and hoped I hadn't given myself away.

"Hardly likely is it?" she smiled spitefully, "A man like Armand, knowing someone like you?" I could feel her eyes wandering over my dark brown hair, big black glasses, and dull grey suit. I felt extremely uncomfortable being given the once over by this elegant but bitchy aristocratic woman.

The way she looked down her nose at me made me feel small, insignificant, any confidence I had I felt drain through my feet.

"Why did you hide from him?" Dorcas watched my face.

"Pardon?"

"You hid in the old stables, I went into the kitchen to get another drink and I saw you on the CCTV." she sighed, "We have cameras everywhere you know, our horses are priceless and so are our dogs."

"I didn't know he thought he knew me." I lied, "I thought he was coming on to me."

"Really?" She looked me up and down. "Coming on to you?"

I felt myself shrivelling inside and getting really angry -if only she knew who I was - what I was. I bit my lip. Marjorie and Toby were waving at me.

"Those two." Dorcas Fellowes Hart looked across and waved to my friends. "Don't trust them." Acid spilt, she walked away.

That confused me, they were the only two people who had shown me any kindness and offered me help since I moved to Overdown, and now I was told not to trust them.

"Are you all right Hilary?" Marjorie tried to put her arm around me but I stepped away from her embrace. I was white-faced and shaking. "Poisonous old bitch," was all I could say.

Marjorie and Toby exchanged a knowing look.

"Do you want to come back to my house and have a coffee and calm down a bit?" Marjorie asked.

"No." I snapped wiping angry tears from my eyes. "No thanks, I think I'll go where there's noise and people and where I don't have to think." I got into my car and drove the 400 yards into the Red Lion car park.

The pub was dark, a log fire burnt in the grate, brasses hung from the ceiling beams, and the oak topped tables shone in the sunlight from the windows, showing years of polishing. Little particles of dust sparkled in the bright sun dancing their way into the room. Red and black beer mats were scattered across the dark shiny tabletops. In the bay window staring out into the street was Colonel Constable sipping a malt whiskey.

"Can I join you?" I asked.

"Want a drink?"

"I've ordered a coffee." I said sitting down opposite him.

"That's not a drink." he waved to the barman who put a shot of malt whiskey into my coffee. "Well, I suppose the sun's over the yardarm." I looked at the yellowing clock over the fire, it was getting on for three."

"Funeral eh?" he said gruffly. "Bet the old bitch was in her element was she?" he shifted in his chair as my coffee was brought across. "Think she'd have been happier if it was me."

"I don't know," I said truthfully, "But she has a way with words, I'll give her that." I sipped the bittersweet coffee and felt the warmth of the whiskey run through me. I suddenly realised that all I'd had to eat today was a bacon bagel and a few dead things on sticks at the funeral. I was starving.

"Can I have a menu?" I waved at the barman and he brought one over.

"Her food as good as ever?" The Colonel guffawed.

I was getting a bit drunk after all the sherry and wine at the funeral, the whiskey had pushed it over the top,so I became emboldened. "If you don't mind me saying so, it's all a bit incestuous this village, you married to Lady Dorcas, she married to Reverend Hart, you married to Christine West, who then has an affair with the dear Reverend." I scanned the menu, I needed stodge to soak up the alcohol, so I ordered french bread with ham and cheese.

"Nosey aren't you?" he waved a single finger backwards at the barman and another whiskey appeared at the table. "But not that clever." he smiled.

"I was Richard Hart's commanding officer in the Falklands, and he was then as he is now, apologies, was now. Charming, influencial, one for the ladies, but a disobedient bastard, always thinking he knew best. We were at school together you know, Sandhurst and before that Eton."

I could see his eyes staring into the past watching memories I couldn't see.

He sighed. "I had to discipline him more than once, but I was always in the wrong apparently."

He sipped his whiskey, "He was reckless and adventurous, and if he hadn't constantly led his men into danger, he wouldn't have had to keep rescuing them, earning a DSO and Bar for good measure."

My food arrived and I tore the bread into pieces and shoved it into my mouth as I listened, the Colonel's face was reddening. "He made my life a bloody misery. I left the army and Hart behind, came back to the old homestead and my childhood sweetheart Dorkie and baby Jimbo, bred horses, hunted, had a good life until Hart showed up again 12 years later."

The pub was getting more crowded a coach had come into Overdown and there was a huge level of background chatter.

"Charmed the pants of Dorkie – literally. He didn't want Jimbo so I took him.

Christine, always the full name for her, was a good mother to the boy." He smiled bitterly. "But you were right about him, he resented not living at the manor, he didn't realise it was her, not me, was the cause of all this. So he hated Christine from the moment we got together, strangely he chose to follow in her footsteps." He laughed, "badly I might add."

The warmth of the fire and full of food combined with the background hubbub of conversation was making me sleepy. I rubbed my fingers across my eyes moving my glasses up my nose. I looked over at the Colonel who had tears in his eyes. "It wasn't enough for him, he had to take Christine as well." He pretended to cough and brought out a huge handkerchief and wiped his face with it. "So now you know."

"Yes." I said softly watching his face, "so now I know."

The sun was dropping into the horizon and the pub got even darker, the odd ray of sunshine flickered through the windows.

"Why should I not trust the Crawleys?" I asked.

"Did she tell you that?" he smiled as I looked at him hoping he would answer me.

"Her husband was known as Creepy Crawley, and he was after anything in a skirt, died of a heart attack having a just legal teenager in a car in a lane on the way out of town."

"Not my lane?" I gulped down a piece of bread and ham.

He laughed. "Not your lane, but the family paid the price for years. The lad is a good lad, he's worked for me in the past, done a good job, and Marjorie she stuck it out, good old stick, took them years to get over it."

He reached into his pocket and handed me two house keys. "Still on for Wednesday?"

"Yes." I'd all but forgotten.

" I'll meet you there – if you can sort out the paperwork and let my cleaning lady Doris in, she'll take the clothes." He coughed, "Well well, that's enough of that." I could see tears running down his sunburnt face.

Embarrassed I got up to leave. "See you Wednesday then."

It was five past five I didn't realise we had been talking for so long. I got into my car and drove back to my cottage – there were no dead bodies or strange old women on my front lawn for which I was grateful. I let the bouncing Poirot out to the back garden to use the facilities, and Miss Marple now called Missy jumped on my shoulder giving me the best cupboard love she knew how to do, until I put her food down, and then I was instantly forgotten.

Marjorie had lied to me.Why? What was all that rubbish about her husband working on the oil rigs and saving up to move to Spain? I phoned Toby and cancelled the building of the shed until next week, I felt I didn't want to see either of them until I got my head straight.

Somehow it was ok for me to live a lie, but not them, I didn't like it.

In getting my head straight, I could not get over seeing that flash of blue in the old manor stables. I went to bed turning it over in my mind. I decided to use the bed in the front bedroom, I made it up and decided to sleep there amongst the boxes. I opened the window a crack just in case anything would happen.

It did.

I was woken about one by a gunshot, using my phone, I didn't need to turn the light on, I crept to the window. I saw lights moving in the field opposite, there was silence except for the occasional crack of a rifle. I needed to know what was going on so I phoned the only person who could tell me.

I was in Tewkesbury in a quaint little tea room, we were playing with each other's fingers over the crisp white tablecloth. I'd phoned him early and luckily he wasn't working that day.

"So what do you think it is?" I asked watching his beautiful dark eyes.

"Lamping." was his answer as our coffee and croissants arrived. He picked up a croissant and broke it and dipped it into his coffee. "Usually two or three men go out together to shoot rabbits or hares, it gets rid of pests. One man holds the lamps the others shoot. You never get more than one lamping team in a field together in case they shoot each other by accident."

"What happens to the rabbits? Afterwards, I mean."

He sipped his black coffee, "They go to the Manor or the Butchers or the poachers pocket."

I munched my pain au chocolat and sipped my coffee. "Poachers? Surely rabbits if they are running free don't belong to anyone."

"Yes they do, they belong to the landowner, whoever they are," he smiled a broad white smile at me."You're really not a country girl are you?"

I smiled back. "I guess not."

Autumn was really on it's way now, and there was a real nip in the air as we walked out of the coffee shop. I felt his arm slip through mine and I smiled. A real affectionate gesture. We walked down the High Street, pottering about and looking in the interesting knick knack shops.

"Things in Overdown have become strange." he said as we walked into an antique furniture shop that smelt of damp and polish, it was cold out of the sunshine.

"Since I came?"

He picked up a bit of Clarice Cliff from the polished wood surface of the table nearest us, after turning it over in his hand smiled, "Fake, but a good one, no, not since you arrived. It's been going on for some time."

We walked back into the street and down the hill to see the field where Richard III had his victory over the Lancastrians. It was quite a long walk and he put his hand in mine. This felt real, this was nice. He had dark fluffy hair gelled into place, wore a smart dark blue shirt and jeans and a pale blue cashmere v necked sweater. Although about eight years younger than me he dressed like a mature man. Perhaps that's what he thought I liked.

It suited him, but the way I felt today, anything would have suited him.

I looked across and caught his eye and he smiled at me. I felt my stomach do a tumble, like being on a rollercoaster. Oh God, I thought am I falling in love with him? Can Hilary Long fall in love?

"I need to be in Bath at the weekend." he said as we trudged across the muddy field trying to imagine Knights on horseback slashing each other in the heat of battle.

"Oh," I smiled, "where we first met ?"

"Why don't you come?" He turned to me and my back was against the gate. He leant on me and kissed me.

"I don't know, I'm not exactly talking to the Crawleys at the moment and they usually look after my pets."

He grinned taking both my hands in his, "And why are you not exactly talking to the Crawleys?"

"She lied to me. I don't know if I can trust her anymore."

We caught hands and swinging them like children we walked back up the hill stopping at a roadside pub on the way.

"I don't know where the time's gone, it's lunchtime already." my stomach rumbled in agreement.

He went to the bar and came back with two hot coffees and a couple of menus.

"I've known Marjorie for years," he flicked through the menu, "Cheeseburger looks good."

"And?" I leant forward across the table.

"Fries." he grinned knowing that was not what I meant.

"Soup." I smiled.

"Bread roll?"

"Brown and butter." I smiled.

In a moment he ordered at the bar and came and sat next to me.

"She's a good woman, she put up with a lot with her husband. Rumour has it that she stayed with him in the hope that one day he'd come good – but he never did."

"Oh." I started tearing a spare beer mat apart.

"Perhaps," he took my hand, "she wanted you as a friend, wanted you to think she had a normal life."

"I wouldn't blame her for what her husband did."

"Plenty did." he smiled thoughtfully. "She doesn't know you."

"You don't know me." I stared at him.

"Yes, I do." His dark eyes flashed at me sending a pleasurable shiver down my spine.

It was about eight o'clock and there was about to be a knock at the door, I knew that because Poirot was barking. Bet you never thought you'd see that in a sentence! Anyway, I opened the door.

"Toby." I smiled astonished.

"Can I come in?" he asked, not sure of his place in my world any more.

I moved to one side and Poirot recognised him immediately and bounced with joy to see his old friend.

"My mum is worried." he said not sitting down.

"Please." I indicated a chair that would take a 15stone muscular man, and sat on the sofa opposite him.

"Why?" I asked full knowing the answer.

"She lied to you." he flushed red, "She's sorry she's really sorry."

"I know." I said softly, I stood up to go and make some tea and he followed me into the kitchen. I put the water in my new purple kettle and turned it on. God I love shopping, even for little things. I got two cups out of the cupboard. I had set my kitchen up the same way as my serviced flat had been when I had to work away from London, it worked well.

"If you or Marjorie had told me, I would have understood." I poured the scalding water over the teabags in the cups. "But you lied to me."

"You lied to me." he retorted back, I gave him the tea.

"Really? When?" I sat down at the kitchen table.

"Well, no you didn't, but you never said anything about yourself, so you lied by omission." He seemed pleased with himself and sipped his tea leaning on the sink.

I smiled, the tea cup warmed my hands, the nights were starting to get colder and I'd hardly noticed after such a long summer.

"Toby why did your mum lie to me?"

He looked into the tea as if the answer was swirling round in the milk

"She wanted a friend, she thought it might be you. You don't want to know what we were called after father died. You couldn't understand what it was like, the names mum was called. Everyone blamed her. Not him." He looked across with puppy dog eyes, "She had to have something to believe in, so she made up that story, not all of it is lies, she will go and live in Spain, but on her own."

"Well, everyone I've spoken to recently have had nothing but praise for your mum." It was true.

"So you've been checking us out." Toby smiled.

"Suppose." I said sipping my tea. I looked across the valley and the lights were starting to come on in the houses, I must have frowned.

"I'm not going to die on the lawn," Toby grinned, "but I'd still like to build your new shed if you'll let me."

"Of course." I smiled at him, "Can I trust you?"

"Yes." he replied puzzled.

"Don't tell anyone, promise?"

"Promise." he finished his tea, looking intrigued.

"I had a big win on the lottery, I used to live in London and worked in a Library in a school there. I couldn't wait to leave, to live my dream, a Cotswold cottage, a couple of pets, to be able to buy things I liked, to have the odd splurge with money." I sighed, "I had a different name, I didn't want anyone to know who I was, where I was, for the first time in my life I wanted to do my own thing."

"Wow." he stared at me, "I did wonder about the money you gave me, but your family?"

I sipped my lukewarm tea as I continued to partially lie to this trusting young man who kept sweeping his blond hair off his face as he watched mine intently.

"I lost touch with them years ago and I didn't want to hear from them so they could ask me for money."

"Is your name really Hilary?" he asked.

"No." I smiled.

"Good, it's a horrible name – how did you choose it?"

"Dr Hilary from the TV." I laughed.

He smiled, "Are we friends?"

"Always." I took his cup and put it in the sink."Same with your mum."

He smiled relieved. "Oh, did you know they found Christine West's car?"

"Oh, no I didn't. Where?" I leant on the door frame.

"In the river." he smiled, "Just by Overdown man."

"Curiouser and curiouser." I smiled.

"Alice?"

"No." I grinned shutting the door after him and thinking it was time to give Constable Constable a push in the right direction.

I phoned James Constable and listened to his shocked voice answer when I asked, "How about that drink?"

We met, not in Overdown, but in Underdown at the White Rose. It was an old pub that had been gutted and modernised, it had a long list of cocktails on the chalk board and a menu of pricey food for a pub. It was stark, painted a trendy greeny-blue colour. It had all the character painted out of it.

James Constable was standing at the bar looking very smart in pale blue chinos and an Arran sweater, his dark blue tee shirt just showing underneath.

"Hills" he grinned turning to greet me."You look nice."

I did look good without managing to drop Hilary's persona. I actually did look the business. My dark hair shone and I'd put it in an updo, it suited me. With my big black glasses and bright red lipstick I looked well, I hate to say it, but cute.

"Thanks." I leant on the bar.

"What would you like?" he asked turning to the barman, who smiled at me, a smile I had gotten used to in my previous life. James ignored the flirtatious barman as I asked for a gin with a twist.

We took our drinks and sat by the fire in black leather tub chairs. I sat opposite Constable Constable so he could get a good look at my long legs in sheer black tights. The swish as I crossed my legs, I'm glad to say made Constable Constable very uncomfortable.

"Well," I smiled at him, "this is nice."

There was a clunk, well, I swore I could hear the penny drop in James' head and his attitude changed. "What do you want?" he said in a dry monotone.

"Well," I grinned cheekily at him, sipped my gin and sat back. "I do actually need to ask you something."

He looked sullenly into his beer. "What?"

"It's about Christine's house, I'm going to help clear up the paperwork tomorrow, I wondered if you'd be able to come with me." The other questions I really wanted to ask had to wait till later. It was like catching an animal, when they're scared you don't run at them. You wait.

"Oh." was all he said and I could see his defences drop a little.

" I hadn't seen Christine for years, it doesn't seem right I should just go to her house and go through her things. I watched his sullen face waiting for a reply, there was none." I didn't see you at the Reverend's funeral." I sipped my gin again.

"No, I was working, Mother understood." he stared into the fire. "Mother" he whispered bitterly.

I stroked his arm, he looked up surprised. "Do you see her much?"

"No." he stared back at the fire. "She gave me away, I never understood why she let Pops have me. Why would you give your own son away?"

Although I knew the answer, I changed the reply to "He's done a good job." I said comfortingly.

"Christine did a good job as well," he looked thoughtful, "I was horrible to her even to the last."

"No you weren't" I felt sorry to have even contacted his stepmother, if she hadn't visited me that night, perhaps she would still be alive. So I told him that.

No, it was my fault." he looked at me and then back into the fire, his thumb in the handle of his pint glass. "I was being stupid."

"Sorry?"

"About you.I thought." he stopped, "I don't know what I thought."

"A plain woman, alone, vunerable, perhaps in need of comfort sex?"

He garrumphed like his father and it made me smile.

"It was stupid, by the way I don't think you're plain or vunerable, now I know you better."

"Big of you to admit it, I don't know whether to be flattered or insulted." I stood up, "Another one?"

He smiled and he brushed his dark hair out of his eyes as he looked up at me. It was his turn to look vunerable and cute. "Better have a coffee I drove here. Have to uphold the law you know."

"How's that going?" I asked picking up my glass to take to the bar, and giving James an eyeful of black and purple lace bra as I leant over to pick up his glass.

Strangely I felt insulted as he looked away. "Not as good as you might think."

"Why?" I asked looking like a barmaid with a low cut frock and a glass in each hand.

"Christine's car." he answered flatly.

"Did you find it?" I asked as if I didn't know.

"It was in the river at the other end of town." he fiddled with something in his pocket and took it out and looked at it.

When I came back with the two coffees and sat down, I saw he'd put a silver St Christopher on the table.

"It was always hanging from her rear view mirror." he touched it gently, "I bought it for her when I went on a ski trip from school."

"So you didn't really hate her?" I asked bluntly.

"I did and I didn't" he took the coffee. "Mother was always in the background, sometimes, not often, I'd go and stay at the Manor, but the dear Reverend Hart didn't like it, I reminded him too much of my father."

He put the coffee down and put the St Christopher in his pocket.

"Yes, I'll come on Wednesday, what time?"

I hadn't got any food in the house, and since the double murders, the supermarkets refused to deliver to me. I usually ordered on line, I really don't know why my secretary used to moan about it so much, it was easy.

OK, so it wasn't really part of her job, but I paid her an awful lot and got very little in return. I smiled. I bet she wished she had a job now.

I fed Poirot the scraps of sandwich meat from the fridge and gave Missy some cat biscuits which she declined in no uncertain manner, so Poirot scoffed those as well.

The nearest big supermarket was in Tetbury, yes I could have used the Overdown Co-op, the deli, or the butchers. But I didn't feel like going into Overdown today, I was fed up with Hilary, fed up with Overdown, fed up with the police and playing amateur detective, I was just fed up. This wasn't how it was meant to be.

I parked in the out-of-town supermarket and as I walked to the door I saw the red Mercedes that has nearly clipped my car and that had haunted me in Bath.

I walked into the supermarket with my trolley, and stopped to look at the local papers on the news stand. Out of sight behind the glossy mags I heard a familiar voice of a woman and a not so familiar voice of a young man. With unusual presence of mind I put my iPhone on to record.

"For God's sake John." Dorcas said harshly under her breath.

"What Mother? Don't you like to see your beloved son drowning his sorrows?"

I could just see a whiskey bottle being waved about behind the Hello magazines.

"Not at 11.o'clock in the morning in the supermarket." she hissed,"What do you think you're doing? Think about our reputation."

"Our reputation?" he sounded sarcastic but not drunk, he was just a typical teenage boy playing up against his mother.

"Think of your father John, I know you're upset but this is wrong." she whispered.

"I'll tell you what's wrong mother." his voice lowered threateningly, "Is killing Daddy's mistress and pushing her car into the river, and pretending it had nothing to do with us."

Dorcas flared. "Shut up. Shut up," she hissed, grabbing his arm sharply and hauling him outside.

I slid out of their sight behind the racks of vegetables and tried to listen to my phone. What I hadn't accounted for was the level of noise in the supermarket.

Trollies clattering, tills bleeping, customers chatting, background music interrupted by voice announcements. What I thought I had recorded was buried in all the clatter. I turned my phone off and shoved it in my pocket.

I bought steak, asparagus, blue cheese, new potatoes, broccoli, I could eat what I liked now, I no longer had to be on a diet for the rest of my life. Strangely I hadn't put on any weight, which I put down to stress and working on the house. I caught a glimpse of myself in the shop window as I walked out. If anything, I'd got thinner.

I loaded the car up and tried not to think about what I'd just overheard. Turned my mind away from it. It was none of my business, just because the bodies of two lovers were found on my front lawn didn't mean I had to get involved did it?

Back at the house I fed the bouncing Poirot and sulky Miss Marple and after a few cuddles and kisses of both, I decided to take Poirot out for his walk.

We walked across the road to the field, it was mainly grass and my little boy had a great time chasing about and digging at rabbit holes. We played fetch and he brought me back, not the stick I thrown for him but an empty cartridge case and raced off to find me another one.

It must have been from the Lamping the other night. I picked my phone out of my pocket and rang James Constable. "Hi James."

"I'm on duty," came an embarrassed voice.

"Yes, that's why I wanted to talk to you." I felt offended, he wasn't my boyfriend after all. "Did you confiscate all the shotguns from Overdown?"

"Of course, and I'm getting no end of stick for it from the locals and forensics are taking their time over it, why?"

"Well people were lamping in the field across the road from my house the other night and I've got a cartridge here in my hand now."

"I'll be right over." he said and my phone clicked off.

When I got back to the house, which I no longer call home for the moment I saw Toby carrying shed sides into the back garden.

"All right there?" I called as he lugged the shed through past the side hedge.

"Toby, look there's Toby." I said as I let Poirot off his lead, he immediately jumped at him and started licking his hands – not really a good idea as the shed slipped and I had to rush across and help catch it.

"Don't do that, it's dangerous." Toby frowned at me, "You could have been hurt." he snapped.

"I was trying to help. Sorry." I carefully put my end of the shed side down on the path. For some reason we both seemed embarrassed and out of sorts with each other. Gone was the easy gardener, employer relationship, something else was happening and I didn't know what it was.

Poirot couldn't care less and bounced around as if he were on springs. I heard a car draw up in front of the hedge and was pleased to see PC Lowndes get out of the police car. He was alone.

"Come with me," I pulled Toby's huge frame into the cottage by the back door.

"Hello." PC Lowndes called through the front door, I heard it creak, when this is all over it's going to get some serious WD40 on those hinges.

"In the back." I yelled. Toby was sitting at my scrubbed pine kitchen table and I'd just handed him a mug of tea.

"I should be working." he grumbled.

"I'm paying you anyway, so stay where you are." I hissed at him.

"Where's that cartridge?" PC Lowndes asked immediately.

"I want to make a statement – get your notebook out." I said passing a mug of tea to PC Lowndes who laughed. "About what?"

"I saw Christine West's car in the stables at the Manor, the dilapidated ones at the back of the house." I spurted out. "On the day of the funeral."

"Are you sure?" he'd stopped laughing. "What were you doing in the old stables?"

"Hiding." Toby sipped his tea, "There was this French bloke she thought was coming on to her, so she hid till he left."

"You were there?" PC Lowndes looked puzzled.

"At the funeral, with my mum, yes." Toby glared at me, "We covered for her, turns out he thought he knew her."

"Did he?" he asked me.

"No," I lied, "But Lady Dorcas told me she saw me on the CCTV cameras, they might have recorded discs – I saw the wing and headlight of Christine's car under a tarpaulin."

"Why didn't you say anything before?"

"Excuse me, but aren't you supposed to be the police?" I asked sarcastically but I soon realised that I'd gone too far.

PC Lowndes stood up. "Be careful how you talk to me Miss Long." he seemed really offended, but not enough to stop taking notes, "What time?"

"After three, sorry but I thought you'd have searched the manor grounds." I sat down beside Toby on the bench and he shifted to let me in.

"I sent James as he knew the place." he stared at me, "I'm sure he did his job."

"Look at the CCTV." I suggested, "You might see it."

"Perhaps." He smiled, but I knew he wasn't going to do it, something in his manner gave it away. I pulled out my phone and played the recording I'd made at the supermarket. On the way back I had forwarded it to London to have it cleaned up, and when it returned to me, Dorcas and John's voices were clearly audible. PC Lowndes wasn't smiling any more.

"Can I have that?" he asked.

"No, it's my phone, but I'll forward it to you." he read the number to me and I forwarded to him.

"Delete that, I've got it now." PC Lowndes closed his notebook.

"OK," I lied again, pressing a random button on my phone that made a convincing beep.

"The cartridge." PC Lowndes held out his hand and I dropped onto his palm.

"When was this?"

"A couple of nights ago I think, very recent." I answered, "Why didn't James come himself?"

"He was busy." he said shortly. I was hoping he was embarrassed that I was solving the case for him, if he was it didn't show. "He had to go up to the Manor again."

Missy started rubbing round my ankles, PC Lowndes walked to the door.

"I may have to talk to you again." he said as he let himself out.

Toby stood up and put the mugs in the sink. "I can see why you wanted me here. I know you didn't delete that message, and I don't think he does either." he folded his arms and stared at me. "I'm going to get on with the shed before the light goes if that's all right with you."

When they had both gone, I did what I always did when life went awry. I got out my notebook and made a flow chart. It was either Dorcas or John who killed Christine. A crime of passion? Did the son cover it up for his mother?

Who owns that red Mercedes that I see everywhere? Why when Reverend Hart's life was over did she take her revenge on Christine? There seemed very little point in that. None of it made any sense.

I was getting cold so I lit the wood burner, heated some cream of tomato soup, and snuggled under a nice wool blanket with Missy beside my hip and Poirot with his head on my lap and ate my tea.

I woke at 6am, a watery sky was glowing cold and orange through the windows, I must have fallen asleep after or during eating my soup.

Poirot's face showed me he'd kindly finished it off for me. Missy was mewling at the food cupboard. I checked the lawn, there was a slight frosty dew but no dead bodies.

Relieved I went into the kitchen and put the kettle on. The day I had dreaded had arrived. Wednesday.

I decided to walk along the lane the forty or so meters to Christine West's rented cottage. It was cold so I was wearing my new Arran sweater over a long sleeved cream shirt, with a lace scarf casually thrown around my neck.

I wore skinny jeans and my hunter wellies that I bought a few days ago. I tucked my skinny jeans into them pulled my dark hair up into a careless ponytail and popped my big black glasses on. I felt as if I was wearing another disguise, I checked myself over, I looked quite "horsey" quite Overdown.

Poirot wanted to come and scrabbled at the door, but as I'd let him relieve himself in the garden, he would have to wait for a walk. I pushed his little black wet nose back behind my front door and strode down the lane to Rose Cottage.

Mrs Weaver and James Constable were chatting on the doorstep when I arrived.

"Morning." I said taking the key out of my pocket and opening the door.

"Where do you want me to start?" Mrs Weaver asked James.

He looked at me. "What did father suggest?"

Father had suggested nothing – so it was up to me. "He asked if you would take all her clothes to the charity shop in Tetbury, not Overdown or Underdown." James nodded in agreement, he didn't want to see anyone wearing Christine's expensive designer clothes locally either.

"I suggest you go through the coat pockets and bag the stuff up Mrs Weaver and then James can take it away."

"Don't seem right." Mrs Weaver grumbled.

"Well then, James can do the pockets and you bag the clothes up ready for James to take." She looked at me and nodded in agreement and made her way upstairs.

"What about the dirty laundry?" James whispered.

"Bin it." I said coldly.

The rented cottage was the same as mine but sideways on, whoever had built my cottage had also built this one. The layout was exactly the same.

The kitchen had white units with a white plastic butler sink, the cupboards had white plastic round handles, an imitation of my more expensive bone coloured ones. It was a cheap and cheerful version of my handmade oak units in white.

James followed me into the kitchen and I handed him some black bin bags I found in the broom cupboard and he went upstairs to join Mrs Weaver.

The house was immaculately clean, you wouldn't know anyone had lived there apart from the upturned cup in the sink and the newspaper open at the crossword with a pen beside it. She had only filled in a couple of the clues.

CID had already been in and taken her briefcase and her phones, if they had searched the place for clues they had left it very tidy.

There was a lovely little mahogany desk in the bay window, the bin beside it had been emptied, the blotter and pen were set out as if she had just been writing. I opened the drawer and there was a notepad with nothing on it. No insurance documents, no bank statements, no paperwork for me to go through.

I remembered something in one of the whodunnits I'd been reading and took a soft pencil from the drawer and gently rubbed it across the empty page of the notebook.

Magically words appeared white against the darkness, sometimes over written but legible. Christine had a good hand.

I could hear Mrs Weaver and James upstairs opening cupboards and clattering about their solemn business.

The letter was a shock it was not to Richard Hart.

Darling James,

I never stopped loving you and I want to come home. I have never been so lonely. I made a huge mistake and hurt you badly my love.

I can't imagine my life without you.

I have told Richard this evening that it's all over, that I never want to see him again. He took it badly and got quite angry, I don't think he is used to being refused. He is a selfish, horrible man, and I don't know how I let myself become beguiled by him.

Please my love find it in your heart to forgive me, and let me be back where I belong. With you and our boy.

Your loving wife,

Christinexx

"James." I called upstairs, "Can you ring your father to come over?"

He thundered downstairs "What have you found?"

I handed him the notebook and saw his eyes redden and a tear splashed onto the desk blotter. "I never knew." He stared at me." She thought of me as her boy."

He coughed and wiped his face with his hand and called his father to come over on his mobile.

Colonel Constable read the page over and over. "Can I keep this?" he asked his son.

"It was written to you." I answered for him.

"So near." he sobbed heartily, "Why did this have to happen now?"

"No-one said life had to be fair." I tried to put my arm around his tweed covered shoulder to comfort him. Not easy as he was a deal taller than me.

Mrs Weaver came downstairs struggling with two large bin bags.

"Shall I put the kettle on?" she asked seeing the Colonel's reddened face.

She dumped the bin bags at the foot of the stairs and headed for the kitchen.

It wasn't long before she came back with four cups of steaming black tea.

"Milk's off." she said putting the cups on the table.

"Condensed in the cupboard." the Colonel said gruffly, "She always kept a couple of tins in case she ran out."

Mrs Weaver returned with a jug of very creamy condensed milk which she poured for all of us.

We drank our tea in silence in the cold kitchen. Christine could not be buried until the case was closed. The death of a high profile Chief Constable had brought the CID into the area and so far there was still no clue to whoever killed her.

After tea, I washed up while James, the Colonel and Mrs Weaver did a final look round the cottage. Mrs Weaver came downstairs with a gold silk purse and handed it to the Colonel. "Her jewellery, it's all there."

"I'm sure it is." The Colonel said not checking. He stuffed the purse into his tweed jacket pocket.

At around 2 o'clock the cottage owner came with his cleaning team.

Mr Roberts took the Colonel aside. "Bad do this James."

"It's all cleared now." The Colonel answered. "Did she owe any rent?"

"No, in fact I have to give you £100 back." he handed the Colonel two fifty pound notes.

"Mrs Weaver." The Colonel shouted over the hedge.

She popped her sandy haired head over the fence where she had been helping James load his car.

The Colonel walked across and pushed the two fifty pound notes into her hand. "For your trouble."

"It's too much." She struggled to open her handbag."I can change some of it for you."

"No." he insisted. "You've earned it."

"Thank you very much," she smiled. "I can't say this won't come in handy."

"Come back to the house for a bit of lunch, both of you." the Colonel barked, it wasn't a request it was an order, so I got into James' car. The back was full of the bin bags with Christine's clothes, and there was a slight smell of Chanel No.5. Obviously her favourite.

I opened the window. "Do you mind?" I asked James junior.

"Not at all," he said putting his car into gear and followed his father's new silver Landrover down the lane.

"Did you find anything at the manor?"

He said nothing, concentrating on the road.

"Did you speak to John?"

Again nothing.

"Are you talking to me?" I asked.

"Not about that." He answered eventually.

"Okay." I watched as the automatic gates opened into a long gravel drive with an avenue of yew trees.

The house was a rich cream Cotswold stone Jacobean mansion and stood magnificently facing the end of the avenue of trees. We drove around a circular fountain and up to the front door which opened as if by magic. An elderly butler stood behind the door, he must have been eighty if he was a day.

"Lunch please Harris, in the Blue." The Colonel ordered.

The Blue was a small cosy breakfast room off the kitchen, it had a large scrubbed pine table about 20 years older than Harris, and had ten chairs around it. The plasterwork had been painted pale sky blue. Polished copper pots hung against the wall over a huge blacked Victorian stove. A white painted plate rack held rows of blue and white Delft china.

A door at the top of the table opened and tea, coffee, orange juice and wine suddenly appeared along with fruit, salad, fresh crusty bread, butter, ham, cheese, chutney and a few quails eggs for good measure.

Harris was almost invisible as he went about his tasks, tea and coffee were poured, bread sliced, the table set and he was gone.

"Help yourself." The Colonel poured himself some wine and took a coffee.

James made himself a huge cheese and chutney sandwich.

I took some salad and a slice of ham, cut a slice of bread in half and put it on my plate.

The Colonel took the end of the loaf and put a chunk of cheese on it without butter or chutney, he took the other half of the bread I had cut put it on top and bit into it in silence.

The house was magnificent. The paintings that hung in the Blue were all Stubbs pictures of hunters and dogs. I could imagine them waiting to start off from the front of the house, stirrup cups in hand, a younger butler with a tray walking amongst the huge Bays and Chestnuts as they waited impatiently for their riders to finish their drinks.

"So there was no paperwork." The Colonel said eventually.

"Only the notebook." I answered sipping my tea and wondering how on earth I was going to get back to my cottage, I'd come out without my phone or any money.

"What made you do the scribbling thing?" James asked.

"I saw it on TV." I lied, "I thought it might show something." I didn't want to tell them that I was reading so many whodunnits that I now thought I knew about as much as James who had been to the Hendon Police training school.

Note to self – don't lie quite so much, you might be good at it but you don't have to do it all the time.

"Where's the thunderbox?" I asked.

"Down the hall on the left, but we do have a modern lavatory just at the back of the kitchen if you prefer." James smiled. "Through that door." he pointed to Harris' hidey hole.

"Thanks." I walked through the door and into a huge modern kitchen, Harris nodded to me and pointed me in the right direction. I realised that The Blue as the Colonel called it was the servants hall. So I wasn't deemed good enough to sit in a family room.

I smiled to myself, if only they knew.

Apart from the shock of realising I had started my period. (I had starved myself for years as the old me, so never really had to bother with that sort of thing). I felt that I was becoming a normal woman again.

This made me think that if this Christine thing wasn't solved soon, the CID would be knocking at my door asking questions that I couldn't answer. I really didn't know Christine at all, so my game would be up.

I returned to The Blue and pinched a bit of stilton and a grape, I turned to James. "Could you drop me off when you go."

"No." he said cutting an apple in two, "Tetbury is in the opposite direction."

"Barnes will take you back." The Colonel said, and as if by magic Harris appeared at the kitchen door. "Call Barnes will you?"

I was expecting a chauffeur driven car of some kind, but what I got was a smelly 4x4 full of straw stinking of cow poo, and a wizened prune of a man who smelt of rancid sweat driving me home.

As I opened the door Poirot made a big deal of sniffing my boots, my sweater and my hands, and as he is small there was a lot of jumping involved. Miss Marple was very pleased with herself she had brought me a present. A small vole with a long pointy nose, she dropped it on the doorstep. I thanked her and she walked off thinking she had done me a big favour.

The phone rang and I paddled over the dog, cat and vole to answer it.

"Marjorie." I said surprised. "Are you all right?"

"I'm sorry," she sounded flustered, "I lied, I was ashamed."

"Forget about it," I said,"are you all right?"

Suddenly there was a strange excitement in her voice."I wanted you to be the first to know, well apart from Toby of course."

"What is it?"

"I'm getting married again – to Trevor – remember Trevor? He does all the gun licences."

"Trevor." I repeated smiling to myself. Of course, he could help me now.

I knew James was covering something up, and PC Lowndes was no better. Trevor became the go to guy. The floods of panic of being found out started to subside. "Congratulations." I smiled down the phone, to both of us, I've got another lead and you've got a good man. But I didn't actually say that out loud.

I had a shower and changed so that I didn't smell like a cowherd, then drove down to the Tourist Information Centre in Overdown. I paid Majorie for the books she gave me when I first came into town. Any awkwardness soon disappeared when she started to talk about her upcoming nuptials.

"Come and have a drink with us to celebrate, tonight at the Bell."

"I don't know that pub." I said. "Where is it?"

"Go down past the Buttercross on the right, and it's on the lane towards Overdown man, you can't miss it. About eight." She handed me a map with the pub marked with a blue biro cross.

The Tourist information started to fill up, and Majorie and Stacey were soon selling guide books and giving out maps to the coach tour that had engulfed their office.

I went across the road and up the stairs in the Buttercross to the police station. Looking at my watch I knew that both PCs would be out, but perhaps Trevor would be there.

I opened the door and Trevor came straight across to the strengthened glass window. I opened the palm of my hand and dropped the second cartridge Poirot had found into the metal tray under the glass window.

"Where did you get this?" Trevor asked surprised.

"Someone was lamping in the field opposite my house a few nights ago. My dog found it."

He stared at me, "That's impossible I have all the firearms in the area."

"This is the second one, I gave the first to PC Constable." I watched Trevor go red from the neck up.

"How long ago?"

"Must be three days now." I answered innocently,

"I've not seen this one before." he seemed cross. "When did you say you handed this in?"

"I told you, three days ago, the day after the lamping." Now I was getting cross, "I thought you had all the shotguns."

"So did I." Trevor opened the door to the office and beckoned me in. I followed him into the back room he was using as his office.

"It's from the Manor, it must be, it's their land." He rifled through some print outs."Buggers obviously thought the law doesn't apply to them."

I was going out on a limb now, so I played him the recording and told him how I got it.

"Lets go up to the Manor." he said brusquely, "Now."

"What about evidence?" I asked,"One cartridge doesn't make a murder."

"This one does." He pointed to the cartridge I had brought, "See that oil on there?" He picked up a black and white photo and showed it to me, I couldn't quite make out what it was, but there was a cartridge with the same stain visable, and the marks matched exactly.

"What was that you just showed me in that photo?"

"Christine's skull, the entry point and the cartridge that caused it."

"Oh." I said. I must have gone a pale shade of green because he dragged me out of the office, and pushed me downstairs into the fresh air. I heard the door automatically lock behind us.

"I've heard how you like to chuck up on coppers." he said as he pulled me into the street.

Under the Buttercross was cool and he left me leaning on one of the ancient pillars and rushed back to the office to make a call. There was a stiff breeze coming up the hill and by the time he came back I was back to normal.

"Come on then." he said walking briskly across the road towards the Manor Gates. I had to run to keep up.

"Bit late for entry Trev." the chubby man in the ticket hut joked.

"Just going up to see old Buxton." Trevor answered dragging me through with him.

"He's in the backs – staff meeting." he shouted after us.

Old Buxton wasn't in the backs, he was sitting in the lounge of the private wing with Colonel Constable, James Constable, Dorcas Fellowes-Hart and her son the chinless wonder John.

Although we saw them, they didn't seem to notice us, and we stopped outside a Jacobean stone window, overgrown with pink roses now past their best. There was a loud hum from the bees in the flowers, and the window was open.

"You'll be all right." James Constable was saying, "you can't be put in prison for being stupid."

"What about me?" Said a wizened countryman in tweeds, his flat cap on his lap. "I helped him."

"So you should." Lady Dorcas retorted, "he's going to be the next Lord."

"Excuse me mother." James Constable's dark eyes flashed. "I'm the first born and you can't put me away without an act of parliament." His handsome face was flushed red with anger.

"Oh Jamie, don't pretend you're interested, you never have been." She stared at the Colonel, and I thought for a moment that her face fleetingly softened, but she was soon back to the tough Ladyship.

The bees buzzed so loudly that I thought they'd hear them and shut the window.

"Dorcas." The Colonel barked, "For God's sake, your son murdered my wife. By accident, I grant you, but if you think I'm going to stand by and let that idiot boy." He pointed at John," Get away with murder, you are very much mistaken."

"James." Dorcas said acidly, "Your wife stole my husband remember?"

"It was the other way round, you're just too proud to admit it." James senior barked."He left you for a younger woman."

"He didn't leave." Dorcas bit her lip to stop it quivering.

"No, because she sent him packing." The Colonel leant forward to pick up a drink of water."He wouldn't have left anyway because he knew he was on to a good thing here financially." The Colonel was on a roll, "Poor Christine was just a bit of fun for him. God knows I bet he got none at home."

"Give it to her Colonel." I whispered.

Trevor put his hand over my mouth and immediately got stung by a bee.

He backed quietly away from the window and plunged his hand into the cold water of the fountain.

Quite brave I thought, I'd have been jumping round shouting fuck, fuck, fuck.

"What's going to happen to me?" John junior asked through the argument. "I can't go to prison."

"No you won't." Jame Constable looked at his stepbrother kindly, "If we get it right you'll get a suspended sentence for reckless murder."

"Why are you helping him?" asked the Colonel.

James looked across at his mother who turned her elegant well groomed head away from him.

"I don't know." he said watching her cold face.

Trevor pulled at my arm and we walked into the Manor through a huge wooden back door. Trevor obviously knew his way about. He also knew he had back up, something I wasn't aware of when I whispered in his ear.

"You must be joking." He stared at me incredulously.

"No," I smiled, "I've always wanted to so this, and I think I know how it happened."

Trevor shrugged his shoulders. "You might as well, it'll buy me some time, I'll come in when I hear them laughing."

I didn't knock, I reached out and opened the elegant double doors and closed them smartly behind me.

"Hilary? Who let you in?" asked James junior.

"Get out," snapped Dorcas, "Get out."

"Now, now," I smiled at her, "I'm going to tell you how Christine died and who killed her, don't you want to know?" I pulled myself up to my full height and leant on the double doors so that no-one could get past me. But no-one even moved.

I felt a thrill I had not felt since I left the Boardrooms of London, my heart was pounding, always did when I was preparing myself for battle.

"For God's sake don't be so ridiculous." Dorcas snapped at me. "This isn't some Miss Marple episode. This is real life."

"Is it?" I smiled, I could feel my old self bubbling to the fore, the savvy tough businesswoman who knew everything. Yes everything.

"Well, bear with me folks while I put this together for you." I shoved my hands in my jeans pocket and switched my trusty iPhone on to record.

"James, James." I smiled condescendingly at the young policeman. "There's no use trying to get this woman to love you. She never will, not even saving her chinless wonder of a son from prison will do that."

Dorcas' mouth fell open as if to speak but she said nothing.

"Now what should have happened Buxton, when John shot Christine by accident, is that you should have called the police. Not the toy town police from here, but Tetbury." I looked at James junior, "Sorry James."

He shrugged his shoulders in agreement.

"She might have been saved if you had called an ambulance as well." I turned on Buxton fiercely. "What were you thinking?"

He stood up to leave.

"Sit down." I barked at him, my voice changed, deeper more authoritative. "I'm not finished yet."

He remained standing and I gave him my best Paddington bear hard stare, and he dropped into his seat again.

"When you threw the poor woman over my hedge and into my garden, didn't you even think to check if she was alive?"

Buxton stood up, "I've shot many an animal in the head, they don't live."

"Christine was not an animal." I shouted angrily at him. "John shot her yes, but you murdered her."

The room was so quiet you could hear a pin drop.

"Lamping, I've been told, is dangerous." I stared at John. "A stray shot went through the window of Christine's car and into the side of her head, as she was leaving my place. I wish to God I'd never asked her over." I growled. My visage must have changed as a few faces in the room drained of colour.

"Her car came to a halt, or perhaps she hadn't started it yet. But she was sitting in her car."

"Taking a mint out of the glovebox." The Colonel's face saddened. "She was probably on her way to work and always liked a mint while driving."

"The cartridge came through the hedge and hit her." I watched John's face,

"I know it was an accident, you didn't know she was there until you heard the impact noise. Now is the time for you to tell the truth, unlike your mother."

Dorcas turned in her chair her elegant face watching the tourists in her grounds outside her window heading home.

"John,"she snapped at him. "Don't say a word."

His reedy teenage half broken voice filled the room. "I'm sick of all this." he caught her gaze,"of being told who I am and what I want – by you. It's who you are and what you want. I'm not you mother." he turned towards me, "It was horrible." he bit his lip aware that the aristocracy do not show their feelings. "It was pitch black, the moon had gone behind the clouds and I had a rabbit in my sights just at the bottom of the hedge, near to the entrance of the warren. I moved forward to fire and tripped on a stone, kicked it in the dark and the shot went wild." he took a breath. "You were right we didn't know she was there until we heard a sickening crack." he stopped for a moment his face reliving the moment. "We went to look at what I'd hit.

Buxton told me I'd murdered her, that I'd spend the rest of my life in prison." his elegant voice wobbled. "I've got St Andrews next year, I can't go to prison."

"So Buxton took charge, told you what to do?" I asked.

"He said that if we threw her over the fence onto your garden it would look like someone had a grudge against you." he sighed."I drove the Landrover back and Buxton drove Mrs Constable's car and hid it in the old barns until we could get rid of it."

He stared at the wizened gamekeepers old face."But that wasn't the end of it, he kept demanding money from me or he'd go to the police and tell them I did it on purpose as revenge for father." His eyes reddened but he didn't cry.

"I didn't know about this." Dorcas swung round to face Buxton.

"But you did know about the car." I pressed her, "Didn't you?"

"What was I to do? He was my son, my heir, I'd already lost my husband I couldn't lose my son as well." Her face stiffened at James' surprise.

"Did I mean nothing to you?" his handsome face drained of colour and his brown eyes pleaded with his mother to say something nice to him at last.

My heart melted for James, now I understood why he was the way he was.

Wanting desperately to be loved by the one woman who meant so much to him.

She stared at him and with sharp distain in her voice snapped the word "No."

She might as well have shot him in the chest, James took a sharp intake of breath and covered his face with his hands. This handsome arrogant aristocratic young man felled by one word.

I moved forward, I had heard Trevor trying the door, he opened it and was surrounded by policemen in riot gear – why I couldn't tell you. In what seemed like a minute in time the room was cleared and everyone was escorted to police headquarters, except for James senior, James junior myself and Trevor, although we had to go and report in later.

It was only when I was getting ready to meet Majorie, Trevor and Toby at the pub that evening that I realised I was still shaking.

Autumn had turned to a cold crisp bright winter with haw frost on the hedges and trees in the early morning. Trevor and Majorie's wedding was today, and I dressed in my best Hilary Long smart but not too dressy suit, kicked my manolos under the bed and put on black flat heeled knee length boots with a buckle at the ankle. Putting on my disguise of my black Clark Kent glasses, I picked up my handbag and headed for Overdown church.

I parked in the town square, there was plenty of room. I always arrived early. I always preferred to be very early rather than very late. I walked through the lynchgate into the churchyard hoping that I wouldn't slip on the cobblestones.

I saw a lone figure standing by a newly closed grave, tall, well dressed, handsome. Constable Constable was paying his last respects to Christine West.

I walked up behind him just in time to hear him say:

"I'm sorry mum, please forgive me." he rested a deep red rose on the newly turned earth. I moved forward and it was if he knew I was there, because as I caught his hand and threaded my warm fingers through his freezing ones he made no move away. It was too much for him and tears dropped onto the frosty brown earth.

"Do you think she knows I cared?"

I wanted to say "Hardly, you were such a bastard to the poor woman." but what I actually said was "Of course." He squeezed my hand.

"It's not fair." he choked.

"No, it never is." I said thinking about my own life over the past year. "Are you going to the wedding?"

"Yes." he smiled a me, a gorgeous smile made amazing by him having tears in his brown eyes. Snow flakes were starting to fall from the bright blue sky. Not the sort that would lie, but the sort that tickle your nose and fall just to look pretty and romantic.

I turned to look at him holding both his hands, "Well, your Lordship, what will you do now?"

"Run the Manor, improve it, live in it." He smiled at me. "Come and help me." The church bells rang loudly and guests for the wedding were starting to arrive, women in brightly coloured hats and dresses and the men in smart suits or police uniforms were making their way inside.

I could see Toby in the church porch waiting for his mother to arrive. He looked strong and handsome. He had a trendy new haircut that suited him and a well cut dark suit hanging well over his musculature. While he was waiting to give his mother away Stacey appeared on the steps, she had crammed her ample being into a shoulderless fuschia pink satin dress, and every ounce of her was trying to escape through the stitching. Although snow was falling prettily and there was haw frost on the trees, she was wearing pink strappy high heeled sandals on her bare feet and her hair was held partially in place by a pink fascinator.

James giggled at the sight.

"Don't be cruel your Lordship." I smiled up at him linking my arm through his as we started to walk to the church together.

"You didn't answer me." he smiled at me through the snow.

"I don't need to work." I answered taking my glasses off to wipe the snow off them.

"I wasn't offering you a job Hills." he smiled at me. "Don't be so obtuse."

He took my warm hands in his and brought them up to his lips and kissed my fingers, then looked me in the eyes. I tried to put my glasses on but he took them and put them in his pocket.

"Marry me, be Lady Hilary Constable, sounds right."

I smiled, it did sound good, but it wasn't what I wanted at the moment, and he'd been hurt enough, how would I answer?

"We haven't even been on a proper date." I laughed squeezing his arm.

"But I have seen you naked." he smiled.

"That's only because you're a perve." I grinned as we walked arm in arm into the church.

"So, what do you say?" He grinned.

"Not yet." I smiled, strangely feeling a pang of jealously when Stacey started chatting up Toby as he waited and admired her boiling over bosom.

"A year." he looked at me. "I'll give you a year."

"You'll be after every young girl in the district." I smiled at him.

"Already had them." he grinned at me as he passed me back my glasses as we separated and went to our seats in the pews.

The Wedding March started, Trevor was already waiting at the altar with Darren Lowndes as his best man. He was nervously looking over his shoulder and finally the moment came, that moment every man should have and treasure for the rest of his life. The moment when his heart leaps in his chest when he turns at the sound of the music to see his bride coming down the aisle. The broad smile on Trevor's face said it all.

Marjorie looked magnificent, she was wearing a cream lace pencil skirt with a cream wool jacket, cream lace tights and cream high heeled shoes. She was wearing a cream lace hat with a wide brim decorated with blue police hatband ribbons in big loops. She carried cream roses tied with the same blue ribbon. She looked younger and happier than I'd ever seen her before.

His Lordship was smiling at me from his private pew, and my mind started racing, sitting just behind me was Adrian my antiques dealer lover and friend. I tried to concentrate on the proceedings.

But then, something truly unexpected happened. Toby escorted his mother up to the Altar and Trevor. He took a step back, turned, smiled at me with his blue eyes twinkling, and my heart did somersaults.

I was truly upside down in Overdown.

Summertime in Overdown

I was sitting at the front of the Red Lion in Little Stocking, it had been hot and thundery earlier and the wooden bench seats were wet. I shifted from one buttock to the other, thinking of my mother, who had told me as a child never sit on anything wet or cold or it would give me piles. I didn't know what they were at the time, but they sounded bad so I had always followed her advice. Now I was just wet.

Toby had persuaded me to come and watch his mum and Trevor partake of their new hobby; Morris Dancing. Yes I know. I think if you had told the old me that I would be sitting in a pub car park watching people with Top Hats and hankies hit each other with sticks I would have reached for my revolver!

So here I was a beer in hand, wet bum, watching about twelve men dressed in white with bells tied to their legs, red spotted hankies, wearing black top hats with partridge feathers in, and one of them Trevor, a ballistics expert from the police force, amongst them, dancing a lewd dance with a peculiar leg opening step.

After what seemed forever they had a break to drink their beers.

Toby came and sat astride the bench seat and put his beer on the table. He had a grin from ear to ear.

"Well," he supped his ale, "What do you think?"

Before I could answer, a woman dressed in black with a neat blonde bob haircut put her green fiddle on the table, nearly knocking my beer over.

She started talking loudly over my head to a woman with an accordion.

The old me would have thrown her stupid fiddle onto the floor and shouted at her that if she wanted to talk to the straggly black haired accordionist she should go across and talk to her - not shout over my head. But I was Hilary Long now, runaway millionairess, hiding away in my newly renovated cottage in Overdown.

So I picked my beer up and didn't answer Toby. I could hear my blood boiling so I smiled at him and kept my counsel.

"Good as that eh?" he winked at me and drained his glass. I copied him.

"Another please?" I handed him a ten pound note.

He smiled at me and as we got up with the empty glasses, the bench table overbalanced and green fiddle and blond bob slid to the floor.

"Thank you Universe!" I thought as I grinned watching her take it badly and make a show of brushing the mud off her cheap M&S trousers. I can't help it, I was evil, but I am getting better – promise.

Toby hefted her up with his hand under her armpit, "All right Mrs Withers?"

She stared at us both, her beady blue eyes took me in. "Mrs Withers was my primary school teacher Hilary. Mrs Withers, Hilary Long of Coldcross Cottage."

He introduced us to each other. She was either botoxed to the max or Toby had been lying about his age. I chose to believe Toby.

She grunted, picked up her fiddle and in front of her audience of locals started to play a jig called Seamstresses Lament. Two lines of ladies formed opposite each other and I am ashamed to say that Marjorie, Toby's mother and my friend, was amongst them. Dressed in brown embroidered waistcoats over black shirts with black jeans and in the case of Stacey who worked with Marjorie – black tight, almost gynecological leggings – and of course bells and brown top hats with feathers. Stacey had embellished her top hat with LED lights.

The dance music started, and the women sang, I had not expected that.

"We are poor Seamstresses, we have no beaus, we will live our lives as virgins mending clothes." was the first line.

There was not one amongst them who could have been taken for a virgin and you could see that even the youngest of them Stacey, with her purple hair and LED lights had been around the block more times than the number 9 bus.

So they weaved and jigged and went to and fro and clattered sticks at each other in their imagined misery, they formed circles and threw the staves to each other. Marjorie dropped hers a couple of times to the disgust of Mrs Withers, who played her fiddle with the sort of cutting smile that could fell a tree. The other dancers though made a big joke of it, at the end they all dropped their staves accidentally on purpose and held their hands up to wave double handed to the audience.

Trevor, ever the gentleman, went and picked up all the staves and cleared the way for the men to do their dance. They circled round and as they went, put their top hats on the floor in a pyramid. "Why ja take yur ats off?" Shouted a man from the back of the crowd. The Morris Men all lifted their staves above their heads, arms up, with a hand at each end of the stick, and shouted together. "So we don't knock em off!"

They weaved, they jingled, the audience clapped, including Toby and sometimes me, but I was watching out of the corner of my eye Mrs Withers, who had cornered Marjorie and was fiercely telling her off. Stacey intervened, "Miss she's only being doing it a month, I've been doing it since I was six with me mum."

"Stacey, go and sit down this is between me and Marjorie." Stacey who had not been out of school as long as Toby, did as she was told.

It was starting to get dark and as I had been clock watching since it started (I was enjoying it so much!) I knew the time was getting on for half past nine.

I stood up, I was stiff, with a wet bum and mildly drunk. Before Toby could stop me I was heading for Marjorie and

Mrs Withers.

"Marjorie dwarling," I crooned using my old voice, "Do come and sit with me afterwards, I think James could use you up at the Manor with your group, especially if you do that hilarious stave dropping thing, symbolic of your lost loves eh?" I grabbed her arm and guided her across to Toby and Stacey and sat back at the table. Mrs Withers gave me a look that confirmed she was aptly named.

Marjorie's face was like thunder. "What do you think you were doing?"

"I was trying to help." I wasn't used to this sort of reaction.

"Well, you didn't, you've made things ten times worse for me." She took Toby's beer and although he'd drunk the top off it she finished it for him.

"Sorry, but why?" I watched her face scrunch into tears and she turned away.

"It took me ages to get accepted again, with Trevor's help I thought I was getting there."

Stacey put a plump arm around Marjorie's shoulder but said nothing. I now understood why Marjorie took her on at the Tourist Information office, they had a better understanding of each other than I could have ever guessed.

Marjorie wiped her face and the dark small bespectacled leader of the troupe called the Squire came over. Her top hat had black and white ribbons around it, she wore the same ribbons round her knees with bells tied to them. Obviously so that she could be distinguished as the Squire.

"Okay for Maypole, Marjorie?"

"Yes." She smiled up, "Just got something in my eye, it's gone now."

She got up and took her place beside Stacey, staves in the air pointing to the centre of a circle.

I got up to go, I understood enough to know that Marjorie would not want me at the table when she got back.

Toby stared at me, "You weren't to know, we don't talk about it, so it's unfair to think you might know what went on." He walked me back to my car.

"It was Mrs Wither's daughter that pops was doing when he had the heart attack."

"Oh." I felt small, not something I was used to at all. I was running the gamut of many emotions formally unknown to me.

"She was fifteen." He took my hands, "After he died, many young girls came out of the woodwork and said he'd done the same to them."

"How did he draw in so many young girls?" I asked, "Surely all they had to say was no." I leant on the car door and fumbled for my keys, as usual at the bottom of any handbag I cared to carry.

Toby was also fumbling in his pocket and he brought out a crumpled photograph and showed it to me. In it a tanned handsome young man with a shock of fair hair was sitting on the bonnet of a bright red convertible. He was just wearing jeans and his broad tanned feet rested on the shiny bumper. Beside him stood a tall skinny teenager in a black tee shirt and long denim shorts.

"I got this out of the rubbish." he said as he took it back from me. "It's the only one of me and him together, mum doesn't know I've got it."

"He's not how I imagined him to look." I put the keys in the lock.

"He was supposedly the catch of the village. For some reason he took a liking to mum, got her pregnant, they got married soon after, and nine months later I joined the family."

"How old were you here?"

"Fifteen – he was thirty three." He put the photograph back in his wallet.

"Most of the girls I brought home he took off me. He was handsome, had money, nice car." he smiled sadly. "All the things that impress fifteen or sixteen year old girls."

"Why did they come out of the woodwork when he died? Why not before?"

"Money, compensation. After that we were bankrupt me and mum." He opened the car door for me.

"Did he leave any children?" I asked and suddenly wished I hadn't said it.

"No. Only me. He was very careful"

I got in the car.

"I'll call you." he smiled as he closed the door

That's what people say when they do the opposite I thought, as I started the car. I drove up the hill past the Manor wondering if I should drop in on James and accept his offer of marriage.

I was tired, sad and a bit drunk, so called on Adrian my on off lover. I knocked on the dark blue glossy Georgian door beside his Georgian shop window, it wasn't that late just after nine thirty so I imagined he'd be up.

He opened the door with a glass of red in hand, and leant on the door frame.

"Hello."

"Hello."

"Will you marry me?" he asked.

"No."

"Will you marry James?"

"No."

"Will you marry Toby?"

"No."

"You can come in then." he smiled stepping to one side.

He led me through the musty hallway upstairs to the sitting room over the shop.

"It's the first time you've been here – what do you think?"

"It's lovely." I looked round the elegant Georgian furniture, set around the walls as if it were still the 18th century. Some lovely paintings hung on the walls, they looked like Reynolds and Gainsborough's, beautiful women, dandified men.

He gestured to a chaise longue by the fireside, Debussy, Pictures at an Exhibition played in the background, a small fire grumbled into life as he put another log on and moved it into place with the poker.

A small glass with an intricate twisted pattern in the stem was put into my hand, it was full of red wine.

"What do you want?" he asked sitting beside me.

"Do I have to want anything?"

"You always do." he smiled sipping his wine.

"I suppose so." I sipped mine, full bodied and warming.

I told him what happened at the pub.

"Ah." he sipped his wine."Mrs Withers is not a lady to cross."

"Explain please."

He told me she had always been a bully, a nasty neighbour, a thorn in the side of almost everyone in Overdown. As headteacher at Overdown Primary she had used her position to her advantage. No one who had children at the school crossed her.

"Except her own daughter." I sipped my wine.

"As you say." he smiled warmly at me, "do you want to take this upstairs?"

"No, I'm not much fun tonight." I smiled at him.

"Have you slept with James?" he asked watching my eyes.

"God no."

"Toby?"

"No."

"Why not? Why me?" he asked.

"I don't know." I answered truthfully, "You've become a real friend and I like that, I can ask you things, I trust you."

"This, whatever we have, is not going anywhere is it?"

I watched his grey eyes,"Does it have to?"

He sighed,"Well for me it does." He stroked my arm gently. "I want to settle down now, have kids, a woman on my arm I can share my life with, my business with."

"That's not me." I watched the ruby red wine reflect the sparks of the log fire.

"I know." he put the glass down and held my hands.

I had been meaning to have this talk with him, but now he was having it with me. This is all wrong. I should be the dumper not the dumpee.

"So this was to be a goodbye shag?"

"Not how I'd have put it."

"How would you have put it?"

He smiled, "we can still be friends, but no sex. I can still be your go-to guy."

"Thanks? " I looked into my wine puzzled.

"Have you met someone?"

"Not yet, but I have to clear the way if you see what I mean."

"I'd better go." I stood up. Strangely I didn't feel as upset as I felt I should have. I realised then that Adrian had been brave enough to do the right thing.

This night was getting worse and worse and I felt I'd better go home before anything else happened. The last thing I wanted was to drive home and find a couple of dead bodies on the lawn like last year.

I drove up towards my cottage at the top of the hill. I opened the door and Poirot my little terrier bounced hello at me with a few sharp barks for good measure. I'd taken him out before I left, but I let him into the back garden for a quick pee before I went to bed. Missy was growing into a lanky teenager of a cat, she bolted her food as soon as I put it down, and ran upstairs quickly, soon I heard her retching. "Not the bed, not the bed, I'm really tired." I shouted as I ran upstairs as fast as I could go.

She produced a nice black sticky hairball in the spare bedroom just on the edge of the new cream carpet, pleased with herself she hurtled past me and out of the cat flap.

I went to the bathroom, wet some toilet roll and got rid of the hairball. As I stood up I saw car lights in the lane, so I went to the window to look out. A dirty grey Land Rover was speeding up to the top of the hill. Suddenly there was an enormous crash as it side-swiped my 4x4 and sped off down the other side of hill. What the fuck?

It was so fast I couldn't get the registration, it was dark as well so that didn't help.

My blood was boiling when I phoned the Police. PC Lowndes had recently been given the promotion that Constable Constable had declined so that he could take up his proper career as Lord of the Manor, so there were two new cops in town.

"Constable Whalley."

Aptly named I thought,"My name is Hil..."

"Hilary Long, yes."

"I want to report..."

"A dead body in your front garden?" Constable Whalley's voice was a dry and humourless monotone.

"No."

"Well that makes a change, how can I help?"

"Someone has just side-swiped my car, it's a right mess. It was parked outside as usual and someone deliberately side-swiped it."

"Is anyone hurt, are you hurt?" he asked uninterestedly.

"No."

"Well, it's a job for the insurance assessors not the police."

"Hang on a minute – they did this on purpose." I was furious and my voice was breaking with anger.

"Probably a drink driver." he droned, "It's that time of night, did you get a registration?"

"No, but it was a grey Land rover."

"Which model?"

"Don't know.. Looked old."

He actually yawned down the phone, "Get in touch with your insurers in the morning, there's nothing we can do."

"Look for an old grey land rover with dark blue paint and a battered nearside wing?" I suggested.

"Goodnight Ms Long." He put the phone down.

By this time I wanted the night to end, I let Poirot in. Fell face down on my bed fully clothed and fell asleep.

I awoke stiff and with a bit of a hangover, those real ales are pigs for that.

I couldn't feel my legs, but the panic subsided when I saw Poirot was lying across one and Missy over the other. I picked up my iphone and looked at the time 7am.

I got up gingerly removing cat and dog and went into the bathroom. After a shower, a clean set of jeans and a nice white shirt, I felt better. I made myself some tea and phoned the insurance company. They said they'd send someone over after two this afternoon.

I got Poirot's lead and tried to put it on as he leaped about. The sun was up, cold and watery, making streaks of the pink and blue clouds. It was chilly so I put on my fleece, and Poirot and I started walking down the lane while I tried to work out what happened between me and my friends last night.

The warmth of the sun was really coming through by the time Poirot and I returned to the cottage, I had taken my fleece off and tied the arms round my waist. Toby was leaning against the gate staring at the view.

My immediate thought was that he'd come to give me my keys back. The work was all finished now, the cottage looked brilliant, if I do say so myself.

There really was nothing more for him to do.

"Hi." I said cagily.

"What happened to the car?"

"It got side-swiped by a Land Rover last night." I undid Poirot's lead and he rushed past me into the house to gulp as much water as he could as noisily as he could.

"Were you in it?"

"No."

"So," he sighed, "It was just a warning then."

"Mrs Withers?"

"It's just up her street." He walked to the cupboard and started making tea for us both, as he usually did just before he started work on cottage.

"You said last night you'd call me." I looked at him.

"I did, but you were out – where did you go? I was worried you were a bit drunk."

"I went round to Adrian." I was relieved that when Toby said he'd call me he actually meant he'd call me. Country folk eh?

"Oh." he said nothing else, but I thought I saw a smile crinkle across his lips.

He handed me my tea. "Do you want your keys back?"

"Not yet, when I put the house on the market I'll get them off you." I grabbed a biscuit from the tin and offered him one.

"Selling up?" he swallowed the biscuit like a tablet. "Moving away?"

"No, no." I smiled, he seemed genuinely concerned. "I'm going to sell this one and buy another one – a bigger one – and do it up. Are you up for the job?"

I watched his face relax and he took a gulp of his tea. "Why?"

"Silly question. Money. Hopefully I can sell this one at a profit, and do the same with the next."

"You have money." he smiled, "I'm not saying I won't do it, I like working for you, but I thought you liked it up here."

"So I do, nice view, pretty cottage, but not the memories, two dead bodies on my lawn in the same amount of days." I sipped my tea thoughtfully.

"If you live off money in bulk it soon disappears, speculate to accumulate."

"Okay. I'm in." he grinned.

And so it began. What was that exactly? Strangely a new business. After much discussion with Toby I decided to stay in my cottage. It was exactly how I wanted it, perfect in every detail right down to the brass door knobs on the light oak doors. We talked for a couple of hours, I could hear his stomach start to grumble.

"When do you want to start?" Toby asked reaching for another biscuit.

"Have you got much on? Because I have to look at a few places first – do you want to come with?"

"No, you know what you're doing, and anyway his Lordship has offered me work at the Manor and I can't turn it down." He grinned, "Never know I might impress him!"

"I'm sure," I stared at him as he went to my bread bin and took out some bread and popped in the toaster.

"Want some?" he smiled flicking the switch on the kettle, "Tea or coffee?"

"Yes, and tea," I went to the larder, now came the acid test to see if he was the man for me. "Marmite or jam?"

"Marmite." He smiled pouring the hot water on the tea bags.

Yes I thought, yes, he likes Marmite!

We sat and ate our toast at my scrubbed pine table and drank our tea, strong builders tea, "Marjorie, is she all right with me?"

"Yeah, Trevor took her in hand, she's the blustery one and he's the sensible one, she calls him her touchstone." he pushed the toast crumbs into the cracks in the pine and out again thoughtfully.

"I think I'll go to Bath for a couple of days, can you look after my pets?"

"Who else?"

"The cattery and the Kennels." I smiled "That's if you can't. I'll pay you as usual."

"No don't do that to them, they're no trouble." He grinned at Poirot who was attacking the coconut mat in an attempt to get into the garden.

"Keep 'em in for a couple of days just in case." He finished his tea.

"She wouldn't" I stared at him in disbelief.

"She would." he picked up Poirot who wriggled and started licking his face.

I went into a kind of reverie wondering what it would be like if I were Poirot. "On second thoughts I'll take them with me now." He smiled, "Be safer away from here now that Mrs Withers knows where you live."

"What?" I was shaken out of my daydream.

"Get their boxes woman, I'll take them now, fancy falling asleep while I was talking to you."

"I didn't."

"You did." he called out after me as I went to the shed.

Shortly after Toby left, bang on two o'clock, a young man in a navy striped suit appeared at the door. We looked at the car together. "Any ideas what happened?" He took out an iPad and started making notes. I explained about Mrs Withers and a wry smile came across his lips. "We can't do anything without proof, believe me we've come across this lady before in this village." He got on his phone and spoke to the local garage to come and pick up my car. "Do you need a courtesy car?"

"Yes, I'm going away this afternoon."

He ordered one for me. "They'll pick up your car and leave you another in about half an hour."

I shook his hand, thanked him and went back into the house to pack.

The house felt empty when my pets had gone, all three of them. Though they made little noise. I went and packed my cases with my old clothes for the old me, thinking I really ought to update my summer wardrobe. I watched as the sun streamed through the windows and the specks of dust floated on the sunbeams into the room.

I stared over the panorama, the rolling hills, one of them covered with bright red poppies. The next full of yellow rape seed and beside it a field green with unripened wheat. White fluffy clouds scudded across the sky. It looked like a child's drawing,

Even the empty space where my 4x4 usually sat didn't make me too despondent, I had been dropped a cream coloured tiny Picanto by the local garage while my car was being fixed, and it sat in the dry square where my car had been overnight when it rained.

I liked it here.

The phone rang.

"Hello Hilary."

"Marjorie." I smiled down the phone surprised.

"I'm sorry." We both said together and laughed.

"I heard about your car."

"Yeah well, it's in the shop. Got picked up almost immediately after the insurance guy came. They left me a hire car, it's small but it'll do."

"I should have warned you about Mrs Withers when you first moved here."

"Does she have a first name?" I asked

"Yes, but no one uses it." Marjorie's voice fell silent.

"You ok? Has she started on you?"

"No, no, such a little thing to drop a stave, and it's caused all this."

Marjorie sighed, "Her daughter is back in the village, I think it put her on edge."

"No excuse, - I'm going to Bath for a few days R&R, do you think she'll be over it by then?"

"You can never tell, sometimes she's quiet for a year or so, and then something will set her off."

"I hope she's got enough sense not to take me on, I can be a tough cookie."

I said half laughingly.

"Don't challenge her." Marjorie said sharply. "Really don't."

"I won't." I was surprised at her tone of voice,she was scared and authoritative at the same time.

After the phone call I decided to call in on James and tell him I was off to Bath for a few days, ours was a strange relationship. He had proposed to me after only knowing me a few weeks. I told him we should date properly and wait a year. He had become a good friend, we hadn't slept together neither of us even thinking about it. Both too busy with our new projects so I had high hopes that at the end of the year there would be no marriage announcement made at the Manor at Christmas.

I drove the car into town grinding the gears a couple of times and wiping the windows when I meant to indicate. I found having a key less car a bit odd and another weird feeling came across me. I was becoming old fashioned !

As I drove through the town I saw Toby and James standing outside the vets and Toby was holding Poirot who had a bandaged foot. I immediately made the training shoe I was driving skid in to the kerb.

"What happened?" I jumped out of the car. "What happened?"

I took Poirot in my arms and held him close, he seemed a bit dopey, "Lil boy my lil boy," I crooned kissing him.

"Hills," James tried to speak.

"Was it her?" I asked and as if by magic Mrs Withers came out of the bakery across the road and gave me a spiteful grimace.

"She just clipped him, it was an accident, he ran just out of my car and she clipped him." Toby gently took him back from me," he's lost a claw at the front, but the vet says he'll be ok in a day or so when the anaesthetic wears off."

My blood boiling I thundered across the road before anyone could stop me, even the traffic. Cars hooted and swerved out of my way.

"You absolute Bastard!" I spat in her face. "A car is one thing but a defenceless animal is another."

She smiled looking across at James Toby and Poirot. "So which of those dogs are yours – or are they all yours?"

Don't slap her, don't slap her. Was all that was going through my mind. That'll mean police and arrest. So, I invaded her personal space and as she backed flat against the bakery window. I noticed that quite a few women in the bakery were smiling in an embarrassed way, and the woman behind the counter gave me a thumbs up.

"Who the hell do you think you are? I'll tell you! A nobody! A nothing, a psychotic old botoxed bitch! I'll have you for this, criminal damage and now cruelty to animals. If you think you know me. YOU DON'T. I will make your life HELL. Do you understand me? Touch me or mine again and I'll kill you - you dried up old prune." I was back, the old horrible me, the me I no longer wanted to be, the me I thought I'd left behind in the board rooms of the city. There was a muted cheer from inside the bakery.

Over the road, Toby with Poirot in his arms and James in his tweed flat cap stared at each other and said simultaneously, "Bloody hell, you can have her."

I stormed back across the road, whispering to myself to keep calm, saying over and over, I can do this and I will do this.

It was Yoga class all over again, I was never good at it, I had no patience. I had no calmness in me. Even when ordered to do it by my doctor because my blood pressure was through the roof.

"Wow." James smiled seeing me in a new light.

"Are you ok?" Toby could see I was shaking.

I watched as Mrs Withers joined a younger woman who put her arm around her as they walked off, Mrs Withers shot me a look. If looks could kill, I'd be dead on the pavement.

"I'm still going to Bath, I need to get out of here." I stroked Poirot and kissed his little brown muzzle. "Be good lil boy, I'll be back soon."

But Poirot was out of it, his little paws racing across a field in dreams that I couldn't see.

"Thanks Toby." I squeezed his elbow. He smiled.

"What about me?" asked James, a bit put out, so I stroked his cheek quickly and told him I'd see him when I got back.

On the way to Bath and my favourite hotel, I made a quick stop to change my clothes at a service station and drove in the training shoe into the city centre. I was starting to calm down when I heard Marjorie's voice in my head.

"Don't challenge her." Marjorie said sharply. "Really don't."

I spent a week in Bath updating my real wardrobe and buying a few things for Hilary as well. I had been invited to the Summer Ball at the Manor so I chose a stunning red number, fitted and full length. Simple but effective I thought, I even treated Hilary to a new pair of matching red specs.

I loved my new persona, she was a real invention of mine. I was worried that I might go back to my old self who I despised with a vengeance, perhaps I had already done that. Everyone was allowed to lose their temper once surely? Except that I had been so good at it. I had made it an art form. My mother wanted me to go for anger management classes, I was glad I bunked off. I would not have had the spectacular life I'd had if I'd been a good girl and did as I was told.

It was clouded over and drizzling on the day I drove back to Overdown, the Summer seemed to have had enough and gone into hiding. The dark clouds looked ominous as I drove past Overdown man and up to Toby's cottage on the outskirts of town.

I rang the bell.

Marjorie answered the door.

"We're getting ready for the Morris." Marjorie smiled "Toby's taking Trevor's place as he's been called away to work."

Toby jangled out of his kitchen wearing his cricket whites with a too small top hat and what looked like a child's waistcoat. On his legs were leather leggings over his shins with bells – they at least did fit. He was holding a stave in one hand and two red hankies in the other. He had a downward smile.

"This I must see." I smiled stroking Poirot who was making a big deal out of his bandaged paw, holding it up for me to look at. "Is Mrs Withers playing tonight?"

"Yes," smiled Marjorie, "She's kept a very low profile and behaved herself while you were away, her daughter must be a calming influence on her."

"Good." I picked Poirot up and he cuddled into me. "Did you miss me boy?"

I felt a furry entanglement around my legs and looked at Missy purring jealously. So I had both my furry friends in my arms fussing them.

"Leave them here," grumped Toby, "You can pick them up on the way back." He took the keys to his mums car out of her hands. "Your car is too small Hilary and my van is too big, we'll take mum's it's just right."

"Okay Goldilocks," I giggled and Marjorie joined in.

"Missed your clever remarks missus." Toby grinned as we piled into the car.

"Is it the same pub?" I asked settling in the back, moving Trevor's police jumper and rucksack out of the way.

"No, we have to travel a bit for this one." Toby turned on the SatNav.

"Where does it come from – Morris dancing?" I asked Marjorie, who being a history nerd was bound to know. I stared out at the countryside as we sped off down the lane.

"It's from the Moor's dance - it's as old as the 14th century." She jingled her bells and stamped her feet in the car. "A man called William Kemp Morris danced from London to Norwich in 1600."

Well, that's not at all annoying, I thought to myself, imagining a jingly drum beating Morris man dancing through quiet villages in the middle of the night.

"You'll be dancing on the road as well Mother if you keep doing that - you made me jump." Toby swerved avoiding a collared dove sitting in the middle of the road.

"I don't get it." I really didn't.

"Celebration of the seasons, fertility of the fields and people, scaring away bad humours. All that and also a competition." Marjorie was making a bad job of applying her lipstick in the vanity mirror.

"Real Ale plays a part as well." Toby grinned.

"Oh." I got it now, I understood competition and real Ale.

After about an hour we arrived in the middle of a Cotswold village on the edge of Oxfordshire. The cottages huddled on top of each other like people in a crowd squeezing forward to see what was going on. The pub was called The Bell and was on a cul de sac leading to the medieval church. The road had been blocked off with pub bench tables and chairs that had been put in a circle. There were three groups of Morris Men already waiting. Toby parked the car in the crowded car park shared by the church and the pub.

Marjorie's hand went up and she waved to the dark haired young woman who led the group, quaintly known as the squire. She was beckoned over. So I followed Toby who went over to Trevor's group. Turned out as Toby was a complete beginner he was voted to be the Bagman, so he sat with all their bags and possessions and the beer money to guard it. He was very relieved.

He got me and himself a pint and sat down. Not overbalancing the bench this time as the bags were on the other seat.

"Are you fully comp?" He asked me.

"Yes my car will be fully repaired and paid for." I smiled.

"Not that, can you drive other cars under your insurance?" he sipped his pint.

"Yes, why?" I asked already knowing the answer. "You're going to get bladdered aren't you?"

"Pretty much." he grinned. "Anyway - payment for looking after your pets."

My iPhone bleeped it was a text from James, he was playing polo next Saturday, would I like to come?

I texted back OK.

He texted back in a second, haven't seen you for a week and all I get is OK?

Yes, I texted back then LOL.

Love you lots too, he texted back.

Laughed Out Loud. I replied, it means Laughed Out Loud.

Bitch, he replied, see you Saturday. Smiley face. Exclamation mark.

I put my phone back in my bag.

Marjorie came over just as Toby was about to ask who called. "Mrs Withers hasn't turned up." She smiled, "isn't that great?"

"Who's playing for you?" I asked.

"One of the Adderbury women. She knows our routines." She almost skipped back to her group, leg bells jingling.

"Where's Adderbury?" I asked making the most of the only pint I was going to get this evening.

"Here." Toby laughed loudly. He walked over to Trevor's Morris Men and took the orders for their break.

A purple fiddle suddenly burst into life, the folk music was being played by a woman with dark red cork screw curls, wearing a purple and green Kaftan. Overdown Morris lined up, there was new lightness of step with lots of smiling faces. The bells jingled they circled and formed lines, went opposite each other, threw staves, and waved their hankies. At the end of the dance, the Morris ladies sang most beautifully in chorus, about being a farmers wife at the end of her life, it was absolutely brilliant. There wasn't a dry eye in the house, and I was amazed at the difference that one missing person could make.

There was tumultuous applause.

Trevor's group the Overdown Morris Men, danced a wedding dance with plenty of lewd steps. A man with a big grey bushy beard came into the middle of the group dressed in a yellow giant baby dress and they all danced round him. The music rose and fell and the accordionist broke out in a sweat playing for all he was worth.

"What?" I asked looking at Toby who was downing A Poacher's Pride with gusto.

"He's the clown, some have horses, some have clowns and some," he smiled, "Black their faces."

A visiting group with painted black faces, bow ties and shabby black top hats called the Blackfaced Moors danced next. They were precise, and manoeuvred with military precision.

The shapes were pretty with circles and lines, but they didn't have the energy of the previous dancers. No excuse really, they were all a deal younger.

I spoke to a young woman who was accidentally drinking my beer.

"Sorry." She gulped, "You don't mind do you? I'm really hot."

"No that's fine." I looked longingly as my golden Haymaker slipped down her throat. "I'm driving. Why blackfaced?"

"You can have mine, I haven't touched it." she smiled. "It's because it's a way of begging, and in olden times they blacked their faces as a disguise."

"No thanks, I do have to drive. Where's your group from?" I watched as she took her pint and necked it too.

"Cambridge." She grinned, "We're all students."

I should have guessed. "Got to go, it's the results." She shot off holding her battered hat on her head as she ran.

The local Vicar, a short grey tubby woman and her husband, a tall thin balding man stood on the stone steps leading up to the churchyard, I smiled they looked like a plate and a spoon together!

"The winners of the Morris Dance of the Summer are:" She waited smiling to increase the suspense. "The Overdown Ladies Troupe."

A cheer went up, I clapped, and Toby roared in approval. There were several whistles through teeth from the crowd and the Overdown troupe formed up to repeat their winning dance. Everyone was clapping along to the music and the bearded chap in the yellow frock danced round lifting his frock and showing yellow frilled bloomers with hairy legs sticking out of them. His clogs clattered to the music on the cobblestones.

The drive home seemed to take longer than the drive down, my eyes were stinging with tiredness. The white lines zoomed under the car and the humming of the tyres on the road had the hypnotic affect of almost sending me to sleep. Luckily Toby's house was just outside Overdown, it was almost two when we all stumbled through the front door.

"Thanks a bunsch." Burbled Toby, "Was a great evening, stay on the sofa if you want." He threw me a pillow and a woollen car rug. "Mums got the guest bedroom." Marjorie waved tiredly as she climbed the pine stairs. He pointed to a door opposite the lounge,"fassillities - good night." I heard him thunder upstairs as I crashed on the squashy sofa and within minutes it was like being at home. Poirot and Miss Marple lay across my legs, and I was asleep in no time.

Across the village in another creamy Cotswold cottage with roses outside the door, someone realised that the old adage bad things happened in threes was true.

Mrs Wither's daughter, Evie, had been released from her secure mental hospital on parole. That was number one. The Overdown Ladies Morris had won the competition despite her not being there, and that was number two.

She had spoken to the Squire and told her that she was too upset to play and if that woman Long was going to go, even to watch, well she wasn't. She had been humilated in her own village by an incomer. Such was her certainty that they would bomb without her, Mrs Withers decided on some "me" time.

She had watched her favourite films, had a long relaxing bubble bath, confident in her success. Nothing had ever been more satisfying, the Morris would be awful and that Long woman would get the blame. She reflected on her day. It was a real pity that Toby caught the dog before she could do it real damage, but there would be other days. Hilary Long would pay sooner or later.

It was getting late, the sun was setting red over the hillside and Overdown Castle was outlined in the colour of blood. One of the reasons she chose this cottage when they moved here fifteen years ago was the view. Near enough to walk to the school, with a view of the castle and the Manor. She was a people watcher and that was so useful in a little place like this.

Feeling content, she slipped on the Kimono that Vernon had bought her on their honeymoon in Japan twenty years ago. Gold, red and purple dragons danced round the robe. She looked at herself in the mirror, she looked just the same, she had stayed the same weight, even that blasted pregnancy didn't make a mark on her skin. Evie was a determined little bastard, she had tried to rid herself of her a couple of times but nothing worked.

She was relaxing now, what a lovely evening. Evie was out with her friends, she hoped she'd stay out. Vernon poor man, she laughed to herself, drowned while they were on holiday in Cornwall, right in front of Evie.

Now who would have thought that would have sent her bonkers?

It was Vernon's own fault, he should have never tried to control her, who did he think he was telling her what to do? Thought himself so clever, but he couldn't swim, and once pushed overboard really fought to get back on the little hire boat. Took all her strength to push him under. She had to put her feet on his head and push really hard. She laughed at her own pun, water under the bridge now. How old was Evie? Six, seven? She wouldn't have realised what was going on. Daddy just went for a little swim and was showing off shouting.

She sighed.

She had dipilated, coloured her hair and eyebrows, she was now a radiant blonde. She had topped up her tan and painted her nails. Then number three happened.

She sat in the armchair in the living room by the window for better light.

She wanted to re-do the Botox on her forehead and laughter lines, and was just about to start when the door opened.

"Oh Hello," she said acidly. "Let yourself in why don't you?"

It was now half an hour later. She felt herself become paralysed from the inside out, first some of her fingers and toes, numb, unable to move. She tried to sit up but the thump, thump, thump of her heart beating in her ears was the only movement in her body. She couldn't move her mouth to shout for help. Her eyes were frozen in place, as she was watching herself slowing dying in front of her favourite gilt framed mirror.

"Goodnight. Sleep tight. Hope the bedbugs don't bite." Smiled her murderer leaving, closing the door. The latch clicked shut.

Thump......................Thump......................Thump................
.......farther apart now, arms and legs leaden, a mind full of fear, when her eyes became cloudy, the fear heightened. She found she could move her right hand a little.

If she wrote HELP on the window someone might come. It was very late, yes, but the pub down the road quite often had a lock in.

With great effort she held a red lipstick up to the glass and wrote H with a faltering hand. There was no more in her.

Thump, I can't die, she thought I look so beautiful, perfect. Thump. Then quiet. Silence.

"Vernon." she smiled, as she watched her husband come through the kitchen door, "I thought you were dead."

"So I am, I've come to fetch you – you vain old bitch."

There was a foul smell of rotten eggs and sulphur as Mrs Withers headed for her new home through the red glow of the open kitchen door.

I awoke to the sound of police sirens and for a moment thought I was back in my London flat. I opened my eyes, Missy and Poirot had deserted me and I heard them noisily eating in the kitchen across the hallway. I stood up disorientated, "Toby – Marjorie..." I called through the hall.

"In the kitchen, toast and tea." Marjorie put breakfast in front of me. "Marmalade, jam." she pushed the jars across to me.

Desperate for caffeine I took the hot tea and sipped it.

"Thanks. Where's Toby?"

"In the shower." Marjorie buttered her toast and took a bite. "There must be an accident in Overdown somewhere, that's the third police car and now there's an ambulance."

"Probably the M5 usually is." I munched the marmalade it was sweet and spikey and lovely. "I've got a change of clothes in the car, would Toby mind if I got ready for the Polo match here?" I'll drop my little ones at home and then I can go straight to the manor, it'd save time."

"I'm sure he won't mind." Marjorie's phone rang. "It's Trevor, I must take this." She walked into the hallway.

I heard them having a heated discussion, Marjorie constantly saying – no – no. I thought I'd better leave them to it so I finished my toast and tea and called upstairs. "Can I use the shower yet?"

"I'm done." Toby shouted down, "Put some toast on for me."

I put some toast in the toaster and popped outside to the hire car and got my case and some dress bags. As I came back, Toby was thundering down the stairs in his old work jeans and tee shirt as he heard his toast pop.

"Can I get ready for the Polo match here?" I asked, "I'll take my little ones back to mine afterwards, it'll save a bit of time."

"No leave them, don't keep ferrying them about, come back for them later."

"Thanks, it'll keep them out of Mrs Withers way."

"About that." Marjorie called from the kitchen, "Can you both come in here?"

My hair was scruffy, I had bags of clothes in my arms but there was something in her voice that made me go and stand on the red quarry tiled kitchen floor in bare feet.

Marjorie leant back against the table like a teacher about to berate two misbehaving students.

"That was Trevor. Mrs Withers is dead." She watched my face.

"What? How?" I asked visibly shocked.

"Don't you know?" she asked giving me an icy glare.

"Why should I?" I looked across to Toby for help, he shrugged his shoulders.

"I thought so I knew it wasn't you." Marjorie pulled out a pine chair from under the table and sat down. "I had to be sure, you did threaten the woman. Trevor said she died about 2 am this morning."

"But I was here then. We all were." I stared at her in disbelief. My voice had a wobble as I was clutching my new yellow summer dress. The rest of my day wearing it and drinking champers watching polo seemed to be floating out of the window. "I was here, on the sofa, asleep."

Marjorie rubbed her eyes "What time did we get back?"

"About half one, I remember because the hall clock was striking the half hour when we came in." Toby picked up a piece of toast and munched it.

"I went straight up."

"So did I, but I was a bit ahead of you." Marjorie looked at me.

"I was asleep as soon as my head hit the pillow." I picked Missy up and hugged her starting to feel a bit uneasy.

"Did you go out again?" she asked me.

"She didn't."

"How did you know? Did you two?" Marjorie's face twisted in distaste, she seemed more shocked that I might have slept with her son than that I could have murdered Mrs Withers.

"I sleep above the lounge mum, and I lay there for ages listening to her snoring. Boy does she snore, and she didn't stop until I came down and turned her over at half two." He laughed.

"I don't snore." I snapped offended, "Do I? I didn't even realise you came down."

"No, you were so tired you were out of it. Do you know you sleep with your mouth open."

I pictured it in my minds eye. "Stop it." I said not liking the picture. "That's not true."

Toby elbowed me in the ribs and we both giggled nervously, "Here's the proof." He took out his phone and showed me the photograph.

"Brilliant," smiled Marjorie, "That is proof, does it have a time on it?"

"Yes mum, look 2.30 am." He smiled eating another slice of dry toast.

"What is all this about?" I asked Marjorie seriously, putting Missy on the floor.

"Well, Mrs Withers wrote one letter on her window with lipstick – H" She looked unhappy having to ask me the question."Sorry."

"So the police immediately thought of me." I fumed. "That's about right. For all we know she could have been trying to write Help."

"Anyway Mrs Withers' place is over three quarters of an hour's walk from here, it's right in the middle of Overdown, there's no way you could have been in two places at once." Toby poured an orange juice and glugged it down.

"Is that why you were arguing with Trevor?" I asked picking up my hairbrush from my handbag.

"Yes, but we do all have to go to the police station and make statements."

"So everyone in Overdown will know I snore and sleep with my mouth open. "Great. Thanks." I stared at Marjorie's wry smile crinkling her lips.

I arrived late at the Manor, James had gone on ahead and his chauffeur Berkley was waiting for me with the silver grey Mercedes. I could see I'd got the clothes right by the broad smile on Berkley's face. He was tall, wore his red hair in a tight crop, had pale skin and looked very young. Today wearing his uniform black trousers and a white polo shirt open at the neck as it was extremely hot and sunny.

I was wearing a lemon yellow summer dress fitted at the top with cut away shoulders, the skirt was flimsey and floated round my newly sprayed on tanned legs. I wore a lemon fascinator hairband. It looked like a canary had head-dived into it. I wore a gold watch and orginally had worn my favourite jewellry – a snake bracelet in gold with ruby eyes and matching ring. But it had been made for the old me and was instantly recognisable. So I put it back and wore a bead bracelet of amber and yellow stones that I bought from the little craft shop in Underdown.

He opened the door for me, "May I say you do look very nice Miss?" he was taking liberties because he thought I wasn't one of them.

"Thanks," I smiled a secret smile as I slid across the pearl grey leather seats.

It took just over twenty five minutes to get to the Polo Field. The countryside slipped past in colours of wheat, oil seed, and linseed. Sheep grazed and cows in the distance stood still in the fields as if they were childrens plastic toys. The car was air conditioned so I was almost chilly.

The tall ornate imposing gates opened for us on arrival

"Where to miss?" asked Berkley, knowing full well I hadn't got the foggiest.

"Take me to James please." I smiled sweetly at him. Following the long winding driveway up to the front of a very imposing Georgian house, and then on the sweep to the back of it, he stopped the car and opened the door for me.

"James!" I smiled surprised. Berkley had done exactly as I asked,

"Hills." James grinned, "Looking fab darling." He kissed me on both cheeks in a posh mwah mwah kind of way. He was wearing full kit apart from the hat and I actually thought he looked quite sexy. He had a huge 2 printed on his red polo shirt. Others in his team of 4 were dressed in a similar fashion.

"Hal, George, Akim, come and meet Hils." He smiled waving his team across.

They all smiled and shook hands with me, and kindly gave me a brief introduction to chukkas and divot stamping. Then James gave me a run down of what each of them did on the field.

There was a muffled announcement that the team heard and I didn't. They picked up their helmets and I heard Akim ask James in a jokey way how much did he want for me?! - James waved his hand and laughed.

The afternoon was hot and windy and I spent most of the afternoon holding my skirt down. It was a charity match and everyone had dressed to kill. I pitied the pretty young things in the black Vera Wang summer dresses, boiling as the heat soaked into them.

Berkley wandered across and stood beside me and handed me an iced tea in a Royal Worcester teacup. "Alchohol?" I asked tasting it

"Yes." he smiled,"But I also have chilled water." He handed me a tall thin ice cold glass. He turned to watch James shoulder to shoulder with the opposition, fighting for control of the ball when the hooter sounded.

By the time he turned round I had emptied the tea on the grass and had drank the water.

"It's so hot." I exclaimed smiling.

"Half time." Berkley grinned. "Time to put the divots back into the field."

"Not in these shoes." I said watching him race onto the field and start stamping it back into shape. There was a lot of laughter and it looked good fun, but I'd seen someone I'd recognised.

"Hello," I smiled, "I don't suppose you remember me, I'm a friend of Marjorie's."

She turned and smiled back. "I do, but I'm sorry I don't know your name."

"Hilary Long, and you? I only know you as the 'squire'."

"Vanessa Harding – my husband is James' number 1."

I looked across "Hal?" I asked. He was a good looking chap with fairish hair.

"Ermm, his real name is Harry, we call him Hal at home and he prefers to be Hal to his friends."

She walked over to a bank of chairs, I followed her and we both sat down. "Dreadful about that Withers woman." I said sipping my water.

"Silly really, injecting botulism into her face, what could she expect? I suppose she just used more and more." She waved to a waiter who brought her a cold drink, " Hal said he could have put her to sleep cheaper if that's what she wanted. By the way how is Poirot?"

I suddenly realised where I'd seen Hal before, he was the vet.

"Nearly back to normal, but playing on it." I smiled. "So Hal is the vet."

She smiled, "Yes, I completely understand why you lost it with her, she was a horrible woman. She made Paloma's life at primary school horrendous, she had nightmares." She stood up, "Would you like to go over to the house?"

"This is your house?" I asked surprised.

"Harding Hall." She picked up her blue silk scarf and we wandered across to the splendid Georgian mansion. It was considerably cooler inside and my eyes took a time to get adjusted to the low light.

"It's a hotel and spa now, it was Hal's inheritance, and in the last year we have actually turned a profit for the first time." She smiled proudly.

A little girl about eight, in a cream shift dress, ran across to Vanessa, she picked her daughter up and swung her into the air."

"Paloma?" I asked as I watched mother and daughter cuddle.

"This is Artemis." Vanessa hugged her daughter hard. "Paloma committed suicide at the age of twelve, she was almost out of Mrs Withers reach when she was found face down in the ornamental pond, we've had it filled in."

"Why on earth?" I started to speak as Vanessa put the little girl down.

"What's suicide mother?" she asked as she swung her hands by her side.

"Its when someone doesn't want to live anymore darling and so they make it stop." Artemis looked puzzled for a moment. "Is that what happened to Mrs Withers?" The sunlight shone through the arch window at the top of the staircase backlighting Artemis' golden hair, she looked like a pre-raphaelite painting.

"No-one knows sweetheart," she kissed her cheek, "off you go and play with your brothers." Vanessa was short, dark haired and not particularly pretty, however she had aristrocratic presence.

Today she looked stunning in dark blue shot silk trousers and a white lace blouse. "You were going to say why did we tolerate her here, why did we let her play her fiddle, badly I might add, for our Morris?"

"There would be only two reasons I can think of; not enough evidence and the other is keep your friends close and your enemies closer." I sat in the chair that Vanessa guestured to.

"Yes." she walked to the fireplace and lifted a gold and bone coloured metal phone which was on the wall beside it. "Tea for two in the drawing room."

She returned and sat opposite me in an ancient 1930s sofa. "But there is a third reason, she was the sort of person who divided the village, half loved her and half absolutely hated her."

The tea arrived, brought by a smiling teenage girl dressed in black and white, who plonked it on the table and left.

"Sorry she's an intern," Vanessa poured the tea, "White no sugar?"

"Please." I looked around the spacious room, painted cream, the furniture was mostly 1930s with some nice art deco and art nouveau pieces.

"They're questioning her daughter Evie, poor scrap, her life was ruined by her mother." Vanessa passed me a plain white cup with a triangluar handle.

"I know, I was at the police station this morning and I saw her," I sipped my tea – Earl Grey. "I was dragged in with Marjorie, luckily I stayed with her at her son's house last night after the Morris. So despite my threats to Mrs Withers they let me go."

Vanessa stirred her tea thoughtfully. "Well, I'll be glad when this is all over. One wouldn't buy a bag for life if one lived in Overdown at the moment would one?"

It was a joke, Vanessa had made a joke. I smiled.

"It's strange it's all started to happen since you came here don't you think?"

I put my cup down on the Liberty coffee table saying nothing.

" Shall we return to the boys? They should be nearing the last Chukka by now." Vanessa stood up and I followed her out of the hotel entrance.

As we walked back down the hill I could see the Polo field and James' team frantically pushing their horses forward making one last effort to secure a win. It was a brilliantly sunny day and the colours of the polo shirts red and white were almost too bright to look at.

Vanessa was pointing this and that out around the grounds, although I was nodding politely my mind was going over our previous conversations. I knew enough about parents not to interfere with the way they talk to their children, but I don't think that I would have explained suicide to an eight year old. Having never been a parent I have nothing to go on but It seemed to me that little Artemis took it well. She was obviously used to straight talking.

The other thing I was thinking, and because I am a woman I can think two things at once, was that I didn't really have a handle on the diminuative Vanessa. When I first saw her outside the pub with the Morris, I thought she was one of the yummy mummy crowd. A middle class homemaker with being the Squire of the Morris her only power which she chose to enforce in a friendly manner.

I could not equate her with this mansion and it's beautifully manicured grounds, and the most painful loss of a little girl tormented to death by Mrs Withers.

We wandered to the side of the playing field just in time to see them win.

A huge cheer went up from the immaculately dressed crowd as the final hooter sounded.

James and Hal dismounted their sweating chestnut horses, Akim hopped off his bay and George his black. They went up together to collect their trophy a huge silver cup with a huge cheque that they passed across to the representative of their charity, The Children's Aids foundation. Champagne bottles popped their corks and there was much sipping of bubbly and happy chat.

As I watched the scene unfold in front of me, I could see that this could be my new life, if I chose James this was the sort of life I could expect. Almost but not quite, the life I had left.

Later that night, in the private sitting room of their beautiful home. Hal and Vanessa were discussing the days events as they usually did.

"So Hilary's got money and loads of it." Hal picked up a whiskey and swirled the amber liquid around the glass watching the glow of the reddish gold in the low light of their room. "She's not exactly a looker." he took a sip.

"Neither am I, you married me for money, I married you for love. It's worked out." Her eyes saddened, "mostly."

"Nessa darling, I love you now, more than ever. Yes I did have the maluka in mind when I approached you. I never thought I'd find the love of my life in the sort of arrangement we had." He smiled, his handsome tanned face and his tousled sandy hair made him look every inch the aristocrat that he was. He came and sat on the arm of her chair and took her hand. "You are everything to me, you are a star, you turned this place around when I almost lost it. You stopped me drinking myself to death when Paloma died.

You are strong and beautiful my love, and you will always be here," he pointed to his chest. "In my heart."

"Thank you." Nessa smiled, "But I think that you've had too much whiskey."

But she felt warm, safe and comfortable for the first time since their marriage thirteen years ago. Such an outpouring from Harry was almost unthinkable, the only outpouring similar to this happened when they found Paloma face down in the ornamental lake. Almost a year ago to the day.

Nessa glanced across the room to the ormalu desk in the nook by the window, folded in one of the letter slots, so that Nessa would not forget,was the note Paloma had left on her bed that morning. In childish handwriting it said:

sorry mummy, sorry daddy, i need to go to heaven to be safe away from mrs withers, she said she would never leave me alone as I am a bad girl. Im not such a bad girl am 1 ? you say i am not. I love my brothers and that is sometimes very hard, *and i love you and daddy.*

See you in heaven Paloma xxx

Vanessa gave a little cough and a tear ran down her cheek, Paloma had become part of the history of this family not it's future. She could imagine a tour guide in 60 years time talking about Paloma's letter, she shook her head to clear it.

"I'm glad Mrs Withers is dead." Vanessa said vehemently. "I hope she suffered, look what she has turned me into – I've always tried to be a good Christian in my outlook Hal, but I hope she rots in Hell for all eternity for what she's done to us."

"Not just us." Hal pulled Nessa onto his lap and slid into the 1930s chair.

He held her tight, she was trembling.

"I'm not talking about the little dog."

"Neither was I, Paloma was not the only little girl in the village whose life had been made a misery by that woman. I think quite a few people in Overdown will be feeling how you feel tonight."

"Let's change the subject." Vanessa put her cup down and tried to smile. "What do you really think of Hilary?"

"Well, she's bright enough, picked up the game."

"Simple enough." Vanessa smiled.

"Is she the right stuff for James ?" Hal mused, "He loves her to bits for some reason that I cannot imagine. Talks of nothing else but their marriage next year. It's the first time I've ever seen him like this, all over a thin dark haired girl with glasses." He laughed realising he'd just described his own wife. "I like her. I don't know why, but I think I've seen her somewhere before."

"Hardly likely darling is it?" Hal picked up his empty glass and instead of refilling it, put it on the tray with her cup. He was acutely aware that she still watched him like a hawk where drink was concerned.

"There's something in her manner." Vanessa said thoughtfully, "Gives her away."

"She's of no family Nessa, thirtyish, do you think they'll have an heir?" He walked over to the window and looked out over his land. It was not quite dark yet and the twilight outlined the bushy trees, he could hear the sounds of the birdsong in them as they started settling down for the night.

Vanessa came up and stood beside him. "Beautiful isn't it?"

He kissed the top of her head, "Used to scare me rigid all this, till I got you. Now I love it, and understand why so many generations of my family fought so hard to keep it."

"Anyway," Vanessa looked up at him, "I'm thirty three and pregnant again."

He turned on his heel with a look of surprise and delight on his face. "When?"

"Around Christmas."

"You absolute wonder." He grinned.

Hal took the tray back to the large empty well-scrubbed kitchen. The Aga glowed in the darkness with a grey and brown tabby cat up against it on the rug, singeing her fur. His mind was full of the thoughts of a new Harding.

Noel Harding, Carole Harding, Christmas Harding.

"Are you coming darling Nessa?" he called through the dark echoing hallway.

"In a moment, just getting a magazine." Nessa was rifling through last years glossies piled on top of the rack beside her chair. She knew what she was looking for and her excitement grew as she picked up the magazine, "London Life."

There was the old Hilary, glamorous, different coloured hair, slimmer, wearing a gold full length dress that shimmered off the page. With a fixed rehearsed smile, she had a tall dark handsome man on her arm, the one she missed but could never go back to.

"Found it." she shouted up the empty hallway. She crossed to the kitchen and as she passed the Aga she opened the door with her oven mitt and threw the magazine in. Hilary's old life crackled and burned in bright green blue and yellow. It was too much for the tabby who moved to a slightly safer spot on top of the Aga plates.

Hal was already in bed." Find what you were looking for?"

She held up an old Country Life, "I wanted to see what the old place looked like before we started work on it."

He pulled the sheets open for her to get in, and Vanessa slid her white silk blouse off her shoulders and stepped out of her shot silk trousers.

Her pert naked body was soon beside him.

"If you think I want to look at magazines now woman, you're very much mistaken." he said as he pulled her towards him.

After the party at the Harding's, Berkley picked us up from the front steps of the hotel. James was smiling a lot as we got into the back of the Mercedes together, it was cool in the air conditioned car and the leather seats were cold. He had showered and changed into a white polo shirt and jeans, making me feel overdressed in what could pass for an Ascot outfit.

"What do you think of Vanessa and Hal?" he asked on the journey home.

"First impressions are they are really lovely people."

"Yes, yes." he leant forward and took my hot hand in his cool one.

"Not so sure about Akim."

"Well, he thinks he can buy anything that takes his fancy, and he knows a good filly when he sees one." he laughed.

He stretched his legs out and closed his eyes folding his arms across his chest – I could see he was tired.

"I want to turn the Manor round, just like they've done with their place.

You should have seen it a few years back, now it's fantastic, they do weddings and all sorts."

I smiled at him, his eyes were still closed, so he didn't see me. I liked this James, he was blossoming into who he was really supposed to be, and I felt proud that I was there to see it. It seemed that in no time at all we were at the gates of Overdown Manor, and the automatic licence plate reader was opening them for us. I was looking forward to a coffee and a chat with the new James.

Berkeley stopped the car and got out, he'd seen something in the rear view mirror. "What's that?"

We both got out and watched an orange glow and smoke lighting up the horizon and James was on his phone in a moment.

On the other side of the village in a sweet little road on the way to the school, a pretty young woman called Evie was standing in the middle of the street laughing maniacally. She seemed pleased as she watched her inheritance go up in smoke. Brightening the night sky with a golden glow and leaping red flames as the thatch on the rose covered cottage burned and went up in smoke.

The following day I was in my back garden throwing a ball for Poirot, who was hobbling bravely after it when my phone rang.

"Hello Miss Long, it's the veterinary surgery. Mr Poirot has to come and have his bandage off today, can you bring him about two?" asked a young female voice.

I agreed, his bandage was getting disgusting, it had been covered in mud and my trying to wash it had made it worse. It now really smelt and Missy wouldn't go near him. Her pretty little face squashed up in distaste every time he came near her, he was also getting depressed by the amount of hefty swipes he'd been given by her now sizeable paws. Even I had a red smack paw print on my hand where she'd tried to fight me off as I put a new flea collar on her.

"No one bests me," I told her during the struggle. "Not even a cat."

I got a sharp smack for my trouble which made me laugh.

The vets was the pretty cream Georgian house I'd seen James and Toby outside in the middle of Overdown High Street.

We sat in the white waiting room with the weighing machine and the packets of special dietary foods for dogs and cats. Poirot was sitting on my knee quivering. Adrian walked in with a pedigree King Charles puppy.

He sat next to me putting his puppy on his knee.

"Hows the boy?" He asked in a friendly fashion.

"Bandage off day, " I smiled at him, "who is this?"

"Bon Bon Poundland the third." He laughed. " I call him Charlie."

"He's beautiful, I stroked his little head making Poirot grumble out of jealousy, I looked up at Adrian, "How are you?"

"Fine. Missing you."

"Oh." I didn't know what to say. I'd been so busy I hadn't missed him at all.

"He's your replacement." he joked. "He's fun, good company, and he doesn't take up all the bed."

Poirot growled wobbling his upper lip and showing his teeth. Charlie sniffed Poirot's face and gave him a big wet sloppy lick.

"Mr Poirot." said the pretty receptionist, "You can go through now, third door on the left. I walked down the corridor into the room.

"Hello Hilary, hello Poirot." Smiled Hal, "Lets have him on the table."

I lifted the little stocky and quite heavy terrier onto the table. Hal gave Poirot a biscuit and they were immediately friends.

"Shake hands." he asked, Poirot gave his good paw and we both laughed.

I held his bad paw up so that Hal could cut the bandage off.

"Sorry about the smell, I tried to wash the bandage."

Hal took Poirot's paw to have a good look, he opened up the pads, Poirot winced.

"Lovely, that's healing nicely." He took out some blue antiseptic and washed Poirot's damaged toe with it. It had a strong disinfectant smell.

"He's lost a claw, it won't grow back, but that won't make much difference to him. He'll be back to his old self in no time." He reached into the small cupboard behind his laptop to get another bandage."Just need to keep it clean."

"Amazing what can happen in a week." I stroked Poirot's head. "Last week Mrs Withers was side-swiping my car and running over Poirot and today is the day of her funeral."

"Death by misadventure." Hal said. "The Coroner's report was in the paper today."

"What about her daughter?"

"Evie?" Hal put Poirot on the floor, "Back in the secure hospital."

"Poor thing."

"Well," Hal said abruptly. "We all have to move on." and that ended the conversation.

Adrian and I crossed paths at the door of the surgery I was coming out as he was dragging Charlie in. "Come on boy, it's just inoculations." he was pulling the unwilling puppy along the corridor and we met face to face.

"I made a mistake." He whispered as we passed.

"No you didn't" I smiled squeezing past him, Hal was watching us closely.

Adrian's fingers touched mine tenderly as we crossed. I said nothing more.

At lunch break Hal rang James. He said one sentence. "I think you have competition."

It was about four when Marjorie rang from the Tourist Information Office.

"There's a few of us from the Morris going down to the Red Lion tonight to say goodbye to Mrs Withers, why don't you come?"

"No, I don't think so I'm not part of the Morris and I only know Mrs Withers from her being horrible to me." I picked up my cup of tea and stared at my view. Always improved by not having a pile of dead bodies in my front garden.

"It'll be a get together, and I haven't seen you since that night. Trevor will be there and Toby."

I fell silent.

"Come on Hilary, lets not be bad friends please." she pleaded.

"All right," I said reluctantly. "Anyway I didn't think we were bad friends."

"Oh Hilary, you knew what I meant."

"I did."

About eight as I approached the Red Lion, I was surprised to see it was filled with villagers for a change, the tourists had been relegated to the back garden.

"There was a loud rendition of "Ding Dong the Witch is Dead." sung with gusto by a group of primary school teachers sitting in the corner of the snug.

"Which old witch?" they shouted.

"The Wicked Witch." came the raucous reply. Loud enough for Mrs Withers to hear wherever she now was.

The WI were tutting and clucking on a long table near the bar at the teacher's joyful release. They then fell to discussing their depleting membership numbers, not knowing that the last two to go were both murderers.

I saw James, Hal and Vanessa standing at the bar chatting and made my way over to them.

"Hello, I'm surprised to see you here." James smiled.

"Marjorie invited me but I can't see her anywhere."

James put his arm around my waist and pulled me to him, rather cheekily I thought, but it felt good. "What do you want to drink?"

"Just a St. Clements." I replied releasing myself to stand by Vanessa.

"I think we're all here to make sure she has actually gone." Vanessa said acidly eyeing the room. She sipped her red wine.

I could see Berkeley and Toby in the public bar drinking and laughing with some of the estate workers. They looked like they were having fun.

"How's Poirot?" asked James warmly handing me my glass of orange and lemonade.

"Mr Poirot if you don't mind!" I sipped my drink smiling, "He's fine thanks to Hal."

It had been an extremely hot sunny day with unseasonal temperatures of thirty degrees, the air was still and humid.

The Red Lion was full to bursting with villagers, some I knew and some I didn't. The landlord, a tall thin greying man who had a small beer belly covered with a mustard yellow waistcoat. He rang a bell loudly.

"Lords, ladies and gentlemen." He shouted above the din. "The one thing Mrs Withers has done for me which I am grateful for is....."

Stunned silence from the crowd.

"She's filled the Red Lion for me." There was laughter. "Love her or hate her, she was a big personality in this village and she'll leave a gap."

"Good." Shouted the teachers.

"The cosmetics industry will miss her, the WI will miss her, the Overdown Morris will miss her," he took a breath expanding the mustard yellow waistcoat.

"I won't," muttered Vanessa darkly into her wine.

"The local garage will miss her." Shouted someone from the public bar.

"Lots of our children are where they are today because of her." The landlord continued unthinkingly.

There was silence, I could see anger rising in Vanessa, her cheeks flushed. I reached across and held her forearm gently, she was surprised but didn't shrink away from my touch. "So raise your glasses to Mrs Withers."

Some did and some didn't.

One of the teachers said audibly, "hope she's in hell, the old cow."

The new vicar, a young man with a shock of dark hair, spoke in all innocence. "Let's not speak ill of the dead, they can't defend themselves, I hear she was a difficult woman, but like all of us I want to believe each and every one of us has a good heart."

There was a loud hiss from the crowd.

To break the mood, the Landlord turned up some jolly folk music, a jig. I supposed he thought it appropriate for the members of the Morris. It was the right thing to do, soon everyone was drinking, chatting and tapping their feet to the music without the woman whose wake it was ever being mentioned again.

James saw I was uncomfortable. I still hadn't seen Marjorie to speak to but I wanted to go home. The pub was getting rowdy. As I looked across to plan my escape I saw her and Trevor by the door to the garden sitting in the cool breeze that was starting up.

"OK Hills?" asked James,"You look a bit warm."

He still had his arm around my waist, I looked at his handsome face. He had a lovely smile that reminded me of him. My man in the Docklands flat, grieving for me? Missing me? I didn't know, I didn't let myself think about it.

"I'm going to go home James, I'm finding this all a bit weird. I'll just go over and have a word with Marjorie before I go." He released me and I walked over to them.

"Hilary, I'm so glad you turned up." Marjorie smiled. "Are you with James?"

"Apparently." I looked over to him chatting with Vanessa and Hal. "I've got to say I don't understand this."

Marjorie either didn't hear me above the noise from the bar or she pretended not to.

"We were just discussing our honeymoon. You remember Trevor couldn't get time off because of the murders just after we got married?"

"Yes." I pretended to be interested.

"Well, just before Christmas we're going over to see Trevor's sons in Australia for a couple of months. Christmas in the Summer, I can't wait"

She smiled at Trevor finishing his pint.

"Neither can I, can you leave off solving murders till I get back ?" He grinned at me.

"Marjorie," I leant over to her, "I'm going home, I'll catch up with you later. I just popped over to say goodnight."

"I'll call you." she smiled.

Everyone was so happy, but I felt nothing much, just hot and tired. I headed for the fresh air of the front door. James saw me and hared across. "Shall I drive you home?" he asked.

"No thanks, both you and Berkley have been drinking. I haven't." I smiled at him being all attentive to me. I was suddenly aware of Toby watching me through the optics from the other bar. "I need to go outside, it's really hot in here."

We walked into the cooling night air, the sun had set and the heat of the day was disappearing. Fragrances of roses and elderflower drifted on the breeze over the little Cotswold town, as it lay sleepily on the top of the hill wishing it's residents would go home to bed.

"Still got the roller skate then?" James smiled at the tiny courtesy car.

"Get mine back tomorrow." I pressed the key to unlock the car, and as I turned to say goodbye, without warning, he lay me back against the door, I could feel his strong ripped body through his shirt, and he kissed me.

As I kissed him back, (I wanted to know what it felt like), I felt his body relax into mine.

"G'night Hills." he smiled pleased with himself.

I watched him walk back into the pub, but parts of me were tingling.

I got into the roller skate going over the kiss in my mind, my body tingling with the thrill of it. Completely forgetting to pick up Poirot and Missy from Toby's house.

Toby saw James come back into the bar and rejoin Hal and Vanessa. Smiling, Toby carried on carousing with his friends.

The following morning about eight o clock the doorbell rang. I struggled downstairs shouting, "Hold on, I'm coming." and opened the door to Toby Poirot and Missy.

"God, Toby, sorry, sorry."

"Don't tell me, tell them." He handed me a struggling Missy and I took her into the kitchen and opened some cat food for her. Toby followed me in taking a quick glance up the stairs on the way past.

"You look pretty." he grinned walking straight to the tea cupboard and taking out two cups.

"Don't talk rot. I've just got up, I look like shit." I brushed my hair out of my eyes with my hand.

"Toast?" he said putting the bread in before I said yes.

He handed me a tea, Poirot was barking to go into the garden, so I opened the door, tea mug in hand. It was a glorious day, cool and breezy, the sun was up shining brightly. Peonies and roses bobbed amongst the lavendar. Fennel waved it's fronds in the refreshing slight wind. The lawn glistened with early morning dew.

Missy raced out, jumped over Poirot's back batted his ear with her paw and shot off down the garden at full pelt with her best friend chasing after her completely forgetting about his bad foot.

"Lovely day." I smiled.

"Yes it is." Toby grinned back handing me my toast, heavily lathered with butter and marmalade."Going up to the Manor today?" he asked absently.

"No, why?" I munched my toast feeling guilty about my kiss with James. Another new feeling for me I never used to feel guilty about anything. Not even when I first moved here. I looked at him suspiciously.

"It's the Fete," he grinned, "The Overdown Fete, Mum and Trevor will be dancing with the Morris, there's a dog show, you should enter him." He stared out at Poirot bouncing up and down trying to grab hold of an apple tree branch to shake it. We both laughed.

"Really this week?" I sat elbows on my table looking at my garden, it was really coming on. The trees bobbed in the breeze and the flowers were a mass of colour. Amazing since I didn't know what half of them were or where they were supposed to go in.

"Honestly woman, do you live in this village or not?" he munched his toast.

"There's going to be something on almost every day from the end of May till the end of August."

"Oh." I rubbed my hands over my face creaming marmalade and butter into my eyebrows, Toby handed me a wet piece of kitchen towel almost without thinking.

"I'd better get dressed." I said abandoning my toast and racing upstairs.

Unable to see how pleased Toby was, to find that I'd spent the night alone.

About ten miles away a young woman in a hospital bed in a secure ward was getting ready to see a visitor.

"Nearly time Evie." said the warden. "Come on or you'll miss your spot."

Evie was wearing a shapeless dress of her own and carpet slippers as she walked into the visitors room.

She saw him immediately and made her way over. The wardens stayed by the door chatting.

"Dean – did we do it?" She smiled taking both his hands in hers.

"Yes Evie, it's all over." He picked up her hands and kissed her knuckles.

"We just have to get you out of here."

"How?" she smiled watching his blue eyes."Can it be done?"

"I have a very good employer who has a very good lawyer and he's going to help us." he smiled.

"How's little Alice?" She looked concerned, "I was away for years, back for a couple of months, she was just starting to get to know me again." Her eyes filled with tears.

"She's fine," Dean reassured her, "She knows you'll be back soon." he brushed his hand through his short red hair. "Mum loves her to bits as you know, and we'll all be together soon."

"Really?"

"Yes, really."

All too soon there was the sound of an electronic buzzer and the visitors started to get up to go.

"I'll come over again tomorrow if I can, but I've got a very busy couple of days."

"Of course, the village fete." She kissed his cheek. "I left you something you might find useful for that, it's in the shed by the side of your house."

"Times up." Shouted one of the wardens.

I went down to the Manor about eleven and parked at the back of the stables, the staff parking. I have got to say the Manor grounds looked fantastic, and I wondered why James hadn't said anything to me last night.

I supposed he thought I knew, like everyone else in Overdown.

Down by the lake on a stage there were local indie pop and folk groups playing to a crowd of teenagers dressed in black with weird hairstyles and wearing chains as jewellry. The music was loud and a rythmic thump thump made the ground wobble.

The wreck of the castle on the hill outside the grounds had come alive with medieaval re-enactors, fighting with swords in heavy shiny armour on a blisteringly hot day, the crowds were loving it.

Suddenly one of James' polo friends appeared dressed as St George and there was a hilarious fight between him and two men in a sponge green dragon suit with tiny wings. It looked like the one at the front was working the mouth and front legs the one at the back, the tail and back legs.

Poirot was excited by all this, the stalls with their enticing smells, the people, other dogs, the pig roasting over a spit. He jumped up and down pulling on his lead wanting to sniff, eat, or shag everything!

I walked past the burger vans and food stalls to the WI who were selling cakes and Calendars, this year the gardens of Overdown. They were quite nice, I bought one as it had all the Overdown events on it so Toby couldn't nag me now I actually knew what was going on. Thank God they didn't do a nude calendar!

Brightly coloured flags and bunting hung from everywhere. The Beer tent where local ales were on sale was crammed with people laughing and drinking and munching burgers and pork rolls.

The sun was blazing hot and as I reached in my bag to get some more sunscreen for my arms, I saw a tent that intrigued me.

In red and yellow large print, almost circus style, the banner outside read

'Fortunes told. Genuine Romany Tarot Reader and medium. £35 for half an hour.'

I walked into the white canvas tent. The heat was stifling. A large red and black shawl separated the back of the tent off,there were a few plastic chairs by a picnic table in front of it. Behind the table, obviously in charge of the money box sat a boy of about fifteen with a shock of unruly black hair falling over his eyes.

I began to lose confidence.

"£35." he snapped at me.

I gave him the money and he unlocked the well worn box, put the notes in and locked it again.

His dark eyes flicked towards Poirot. "You can't take him in, he'll mess up your reading."

"Poirot," I said in my best training voice. "Stay." He obeyed and sat to attention.I watched his brown eyes darting about the tent wondering what this was all about.

The boy took the lead from me and I went behind the curtain.

The medium was a walnut faced woman with short white curly hair. She was wearing a dark red and black dress.

"Come in dear." she said kindly looking at the murky looking crystal ball and three sets of Tarot cards in front of her."What do you want to know?"

"Just a general reading with the Ryder Waite cards please." I sat opposite her and put my hands flat on the table.

"So, you have a bit of knowledge, I see, I see."

I wondered if she did. Suddenly she reached across the table and grabbed both my wrists in an iron grip. I felt a shot of electricity shoot from her hands through mine and I struggled to let go. But she was too strong.

I tried to pull away, her cold hands held me tightly.

"Interesting," She opened her eyes and they seemed to have glazed over."No more running away. The time has come to stop running, you have made a good choice. You're needed here. You will change your life and the lives of others for the better."

I tried to pull away, but she pulled me back as she sighed. "Very strong emotion here, he misses you, He is in despair. You can't go back or it will finish you both." Her long painted nails were digging into my skin. "There are new beginnings coming." Her eyes snapped open and she said quite matter of factly. "Lets get on dear, shall we?

She ran her hands over the cards turning them over as she did so.

I looked at the ancient pictures on the cards.

"Don't try and read the cards – that's my job." She looked up at me staring at things I couldn't see. It was if she could see straight through me and reading my thoughts.

After about half an hour I came out from behind the curtain my mind reeling from the reading. The tent was stuffy and Poirot and the dark haired boy were playing pully pully with a scarf that had been left behind by another client. Ramona shouted from behind the curtain to the boy.

"Give her one of my cards, she'll need it around Christmas."

He handed me a card from the cashbox and the strap of Poirot's lead.

I could hear the fiddle music of the Morris coming from the lower part of the garden and walked in that direction. I knew I'd find Marjorie and Vanessa there.

I spotted Toby in the nearby refreshment tent, sitting on a barrel surrounded by bags, but not dressed in Morris kit.

Poirot pulled hard on his lead and in a moment I found myself skittering across the grass to accomodate my dog's love affair with my gardener.

While Toby and Poirot were making a fuss of each other, I looked across the tent and saw the red haired figure of Berkley energetically playing away on Mrs Wither's green fiddle.

"Finished?" I asked Poirot who looked up at me quizzically juggling his eyebrows. "Bag man again?" I sat beside Toby on a nearby ancient chair,

"Yes for both lots, I don't mind,"he smiled, "they provide me with beer and pies." He started to tap his foot to the music."Look at my mum go."

"Is Berkley playing Mrs Wither's fiddle? How did he get hold of that? Wasn't the house burnt out?"

Toby's eyes narrowed and he spoke to me as if he was talking to a moron.

"Darren was taught the fiddle by Mrs Withers, and when she couldn't come and play, he'd borrow it off her and play in her place." He sighed. "That's what he's doing now."

"How did he get it?" I wondered pulling Poirot away from a rucksack he was considering using as a toilet.

"She probably gave it to him the week before she died. She always used to go on holiday the week of the Overdown Fete." Toby picked Poirot up and put him on his lap. "She hated it, the noise, the incomers, went away to Spain to sunbathe."

"She was already the colour of a hazelnut." I stroked Poirot's ears.

"There's no need to be rude."

"I'm not." I answered surprised, "Just stating a fact."

Marjorie and Vanessa hurried over at the end of their set to take drinks out of their bags.

"Having a good time?" Marjorie asked.

"There's a lot here." I smiled deftly avoiding the question.

"James has done a good job this year." Vanessa took a swig of her orange juice, "We were going to take it over from his mother, dear old Dorcas, but I think we'll stick with our current crowd."

Both Vanessa and Marjorie were red in the face from the heat of the day, and sat on a bench nearby to get their breath back. My mind wandered to what I would have been doing this time of year in London, the Proms, naturally, Wimbledon of course, Pimms and strawberries on my rooftop terrace. My memories were broken by Vanessa's voice.

"Oh look, it's James senior I haven't seen him for absolutely ages." She smiled at Marjorie, "I'm not in the next one Margie can you say I'll miss two?"

Marjorie looked up, "two?"

"Yes, you can dance in my place." She handed Marjorie her hand bells and spotted handerchiefs and hared off to speak to Colonel Constable.

"Margie?" I smiled at her raising an eyebrow. Toby smiled silently.

"No." She smiled back, "Marjorie to my friends! Got to go."

The animated conversation that I wished I could hear between Colonel Constable and Vanessa, floated tantilisingly through the air. When the wind changed enough for me to hear it was intriguing. Lots of "she's" and "what do you think?" and "it's a possibility." Laughter and a hug and Vanessa hurried back to where the Morris had started their second dance, she stood on the sidelines clapping.

Hal and Toby had persuaded me to enter Poirot in the dog show. As I didn't know what it entailed I reluctantly agreed. It was being announced over the Loudspeaker system so I took him from Toby's fussing and made for the arena. My head buzzing with so many thoughts, what if I'm recognised?

What were Vanessa and the Colonel talking about? But the biggest thought that I couldn't shake, was that in this brightly dressed crowd, in amongst the jovial atmosphere and the shorts and ice creams was the person who murdered Mrs Withers.

A nice tanned lady with fair hair tried to attach the number 6 to Poirot's collar, he immediately turned in circles trying to bite it off, so I wrestled it off him and wore it on my wrist.

I watched the other dog owners take their turns in the arena. Hal's two beautiful Salukis sat, stayed, ran and fetched to order. Jumped for a rope circle and walked to heel with Hal until he gave them an order.

I looked down at Poirot who, unconcerned, had decided to chew at his foot.

Next was an Old English Sheepdog called Bumble, because she was striped like a bee. She also did everything her owner asked, but at the end of her turn got a bit fed up and rounded up a group of children and brought them into the arena to tumultuous applause and laughter from the audience.

After watching various other breeds of all shapes and sizes go through the same routine, usually with only one or two faults it was my turn with Poirot.

My stomach leapt as they called, "And finally Miss Hilary Long with Poirot."

I had a handful of biscuits to reward him and felt quite proud of him until he ran away and jumped into Toby's arms. Toby pointed him towards me, he came back obviously able to smell the biscuits held in my hot clammy hand.

I made him sit and stay – but it was too much for him – he knew I had biscuits, as soon as I had got into position he started to crawl on his stomach through the grass towards me like a commando to reach me.

Everyone laughed.

Sit to Poirot was sit and beg which he did each time, his lovely brown eyes flicking around the audience with his eyebrows juggling up and down to see who was watching him. Playing to the crowd – I thought – hopelessly trying to get him back on track.

The rope circle in the Fetch was killed in no uncertain fashion, thrown up into the air, pounced on, chewed and taken away from me when I tried to retrieve it. It was a good job he was the last dog on as by the time he'd finished with it and brought it to me, it was no longer a loop but a blue soggy lump.

By the time the announcement said "Thank you Miss Hilary Long with Poirot." Most of the audience were wetting themselves laughing.

I stood next to Toby waiting to hear the results. Hal's dogs won. What a fix I thought to myself – getting in with the local Vet.

Bumble got best looking entrant. To my surprise Poirot won "outstanding character" a new class invented especially for him. At last he stood like a good boy while a yellow rosette with "Best Pony" was pinned to his collar, I laughed so much my jaws ached.

As I walked back to Toby, to my handbag amongst the pile of other bags he was hoiking round to guard, I saw James for the first time that day.

He and Berkley were standing together and James patted him on the shoulder and shook his hand.

Vanessa made her way over to me through the crowd.

"Hilary," she laughed, "dear Poirot – what a scream."

"He's a rescue dog," I said making excuses for him. Poirot looked up grinning.

I felt a strong wiry arm around my shoulder and turned to see James smiling at me. "Bloody good show." he laughed sounding like his father."Well done."

He kissed me lightly on the cheek, he smelt lovely, Ralph Lauren I think.

"Thank you." I smiled. "You've given the village a wonderful day James, you should be very proud."

"That means a lot." he smiled, he took my free hand and pulled me away from Vanessa, who took the hint and went off to find Hal, Salukis, children, and take them home.

"Can't afford it this year – but next year I hope to have fireworks at the end of the last day of the fete." He smiled taking my hand to his lips and kissing it. "Dog biscuits?" he grinned.

"Fraid so." I laughed.

I hadn't realised the time. The Manor grounds were growing dark and the solar light ropes along the pathways had started to come on.

There was a magic in the dropping of the blood red sun behind the dark silhouette of the old ruined castle, the re-enactors were lighting fires to cook their food and the beer tent was coming alive with folk singers.

James held my hand gently fingers intertwined. "Sorry Hils, haven't had much time to spend with you today." He turned as if to kiss me, but Berkley came towards us with his daughter, a pretty red haired little girl.

She was draped over his shoulder wanting to keep her eyes open but unable to.

"Thanks sir," he smiled, "for everything, it's been the best Overdown fete we've ever had."

"I already employ you Berkley – no need to suck up." James joked. "Better get her back to her Grans and bed, she looks whacked."

"Thanks again." Berkley smiled as he walked away through the darkening trees.

We walked hand in hand down the ha ha towards the music of the beer tent. The Folk music was getting rowdy and there was a lot of good natured shouting during the song "The Old Dun Cow Caught Fire." Poirot's little legs were starting to give out so I picked him up, balancing him on my hip.

In a corner of the beer tent, I was surprised to find that a table with four chairs has been reserved for us. I put Poirot on one of the chairs and he put his head on my handbag and immediately fell asleep.

"Have you made your mind up?" James smiled at me. He gestured to one of the bar staff and a bottle of white wine appeared with two glasses.

I took his hand in mine, his hand was clean warm and dry, mine was dusty with the smell of dog biscuits and slobber. "Be patient." I smiled really wishing I could feel a spark for James, but he just felt like a friend.

"The year isn't up yet." I took the wine and poured it for us both.

"I don't want to wait any longer Hils," he looked me in the eyes,"I love you."

The L word. I never used it. "Why?" I asked surprised.

"I did all this for you, I think about you every day, how it'll be when we live in the Manor together." He sipped his wine.

I wanted to run away again.

"Why do I effect you like this?" I smiled trying to choke down my heart that was trying to get out of my mouth.

He took both my hands in his almost spilling my wine. " You changed me, only you, changed me from an arse into a Lord. Look at all I've achieved."

"You achieved it James, you, not me." I smiled. "Look how we got together – by being involved in two murders." I sighed, "It's not how romances should start. We've only really had a few months acquaintance."

Poirot snored.

"When you put it that way." He smiled.

"Not angry?"

"No darling Hils, just impatient."

So we sat in the beer tent talking together as good friends. Listening to the music and Poirot snoring whilst we laughed at the day's events.

I wished I could come to love James, but my swinging brick, as my mother used to call my heart, wasn't having any of it.

In a cosy thatched cottage on the edge of the Manor estate lit by low lamps in the lounge, Berkley waved to his mother to turn the TV down, so that it wouldn't wake Alice when he took her up to her room. He carried her to bed and took her shoes and socks off and her flowery summer dress and put a soft pink nightie over her head.

"Teef." Alice mumbled half asleep.

"Not tonight sweetheart, you're too tired." Berkley smiled.

He covered her up with her pink duvet with big white hearts kissed her forehead and whispered."Goodnight, sleep tight, don't let the bedbugs bite." He turned the nightlight on as he left the room.

At Harding House, Vanessa was on the phone.

"No really, we want you here, you and your wife can have the flat in the attic – it's huge, plenty of space for your little one to run about in, and of course it will be company for Artemis."

She listened intently for a moment. "Yes, yes, but there's more work for you here. Well, think about it won't you ? Let me know by the end of next week."

She walked from the gallery into the snug to tell Hal what she thought of the Overdown fete.

"This year it wasn't actually a fete worse than death." Nessa grinned at Hal,

"his mother had no idea how to have fun."

"So we won't be offering to take it on?" Hal smiled, "Dorcas was a strange woman, don't see what Hart saw in her."

Nessa flopped in an armchair with a wry grin, "Darling, darling, the same thing you saw in me."

"Money!" Hal grinned.

They both laughed together.

After the Dog Show, and Poirot's commando style crawl towards me for his biscuits, everytime we walked through Overdown there was always some one who whistled or hummed the Mission Impossible theme tune.

At first it was funny – but now it was getting wearing. I sat on the cold stone steps under the cream coloured buttercross. Just for a moment, to get out of the heat. Dear Poirot, just happy to be anywhere, lay on the ancient cold stone slabs at my feet.

Since coming to Overdown I had solved two murders, one accidentally, and the second because no one else was doing it. I didn't want Police from outside coming – someone might have recognised me.

The death of Mrs Withers bothered me. It was generally thought amongst the Overdowners that she had been murdered. She had been hated for years by some and loved by others. Both parties thought that someone had stepped in and helped her off the planet.

But who?

The poor demented Evie? So eager to look for the love she didn't get from her parents that she turned to Creepy Crawley?

Vanessa? Who had every reason to despise the woman who tormented her daughter to death?

There were numerous others whose pets had been run over, had their cars side-swiped, and had their reputations ruined.

No Police presence for her. No investigations.

While I was staring into the distance turning all this over in my mind I felt someone sit next to me on the stone step.

Poirot immediately jumped up and started sniffing the newcomer's puppy.

I won't say where.

"Lost in thought?" Adrian smiled at me.

"I suppose so, I smiled back, ruffling the fur on the puppy's head.

"How is Charlie?"

"Look at him, he's great – but no substitute for you." He stroked Charlies ear.

"Adrian." I started.

"I know, I broke it off, I was stupid." he smiled warmly at me.

"No, you out of both of us were brave enough to do the right thing."

"Yes." He moved a little closer. "But I didn't think it through. Perhaps...."

"No, no, I'm a mess Adrian, that's why I can't get involved with anyone properly just yet."

"Not even James?" He watched my face.

"Most of all James." I picked Poirot up and put him on my lap. "His mother hurt him really badly, if I make a mistake with him, then I'll hurt him really badly as well."

"Lets change the subject a bit." He smiled. "I've got a bit of gossip for you.

Did you know Harding Hall have been trying to poach Berkley from James?"

"No, he never talks about that sort of thing with me."

"Also, did you know that James' London solicitors have sorted out the Withers woman's will, and that his lawyer has got Evie out of her secure hospital? "

I was puzzled, so much happening and he didn't even mention it to me. "I don't understand what does that matter to James?"

"Darren Berkley and Evie Withers got married in secret about 8 or 9 years ago."

"How do you know all this stuff?" I asked watching his handsome face watching my Hilary Long face.

"I own a shop, remember?" he grinned, "I have ears, people talk."

"Delicious gossip, as Jane Austin put it." I smiled stroking Poirot who was getting restless and wriggling.

"Exactly, sometimes I can't help myself." Adrian had lovely grey eyes that twinkled when he smiled. I tried not to think about them as he told me the story."After the affair with Toby's father, Mrs Withers had tried to get Evie put away, but even though she said it was for Evie's protection the authorities didn't agree with her. A few month's later Evie turned to Darren Berkley who'd loved her since they were at school together."

I watched Adrian's kind face as he spoke. "They ran away and got married.

I suppose they thought it would get her out of her mother's clutches."

"But it didn't?" I put the wriggling Poirot on the floor.

"No, you see she was now 17 and pregnant, Mrs Withers blamed the powers that be for letting a girl of unsound mind down when technically still not of age.

A girl who forged her mother's signature on the necessary documents to allow this to happen."

"Wow what a story." I stood up.

"Mrs Withers tried to get the marriage annulled but couldn't." Alastair smiled."Your gardener Toby and Berkley's mum were witnesses. I imagine Mrs Withers thought it was revenge on Toby's part."

"I don't think he's like that – do you?"

"No." Adrian smiled his lovely smile. I had liked looking at it and I had missed the easy way we had always talked together. "I don't think Toby has a thought in his head, bad or otherwise." He stood up.

I laughed and elbowed him in the ribs. "Don't be so cruel."

"I'm not." he took my hand and held it. Both dogs looked up as if we had something to throw for them but didn't. "He's a hail fellow, we met, type of chap."

"How's the dating going?" I removed my hand gently from his.

"Awful, absolutely, awful. Went to dinner with this PYT."

"PYT?" I asked.

"Pretty young thing." Adrian explained."She was so boring, all she seemed to say was Totes Amazeballs."

"Oh," I smiled a secret smile I hoped Adrian wouldn't see.

"I saw that smirk, so you do care a bit!" he laughed.

Driving back to my cottage with the fluffy sunlit hedges whipping past, Poirot drooling out of the window covering any passer by with goo. The puzzle fell into shape. The proverbial penny dropped and I knew who did it.

In the cool of the private medieval chapel at Harding Hall, Vanessa and Father Farrell were chatting.

"Thanks for coming across." She smiled at him, "I think I need a confession."

"Not a problem." said the elderly Irish Priest in his thick Irish brogue "Shall we?" He opened the wooden half door of the confessional for her, she closed it and pulled the dusty dark red curtain across. She sat waiting on the lavendar polished seat as he entered his half. Waited silently as he closed the door pulled the curtain across and whispered a short prayer.

"Daughter?" his voice was low and comforting.

Nessa took a breath and whispered. "Forgive me Father for I have sinned, it has been three weeks since my last confession."

Toby was at my cottage painting the front gate pale green when I arrived home. "What are you doing that for?" I asked.

"It was starting to rot, this is a paint preservative, it needed doing, so I did it." He smiled up at me, "All done now." He held the gate open so Poirot and I could get through, Missy was on the front step asleep in the sun.

He stood up, it had been an extremely hot day, he was just wearing his jeans and his muscles rippled under his tanned skin. He looked very sunburnt and sweaty.

"Cold drink?" I said letting Poirot off his lead to jump all over his best friend.

"No, I'm OK,I'll go after this." he smiled.

"I insist." I grabbed his wrist and pulled him inside. I poured him an ice cold water from the fridge, handed it to him and he glugged it down.

"Thanks missus, well I must be off."

"Why?" I stared at him.

"What do you mean why? I've got work to do." He smiled puzzled.

"Toby, did Berkley kill Mrs Withers?" I asked outright.

He laughed. "No more – you said after last time." He poured another drink and glugged it down. "Leave it alone – it was an accident - the coroner said so."

"Was it?" I persisted. Very hard to be persistant when your dog is chewing your sandal while you're still wearing it.

Toby smiled and made for the door. "See you tomorrow."

I was frustrated in the extreme. I glanced at the clock, it was nearly four and I was supposed to be meeting James at eight for our date night. I didn't want to go, I didn't feel like going for a walk to the castle. I didn't feel like doing anything. I flopped on my sofa. Perhaps I could call in sick. No firstly it's not a job, and secondly he was bound to come over to see if I was allright.

I stomped upstairs wondering how far James was involved in all of this, and how much did he know?

I felt better after a shower and after trying on at least six outfits, I brushed my long dark glossy hair and put it up in a high ponytail. As an afterthought, I picked up a dark blue M&S cardigan, as another afterthought I fed my pets, washed my hands, closed the door on the kitchen and made for my car.

I arrived at the Manor at a quarter to eight, wearing skinny dark blue jeans, walking shoes and a crisp white shirt. I looked clean and fresh but strangely not like me or Hilary.

When I arrived James was standing on the steps of the Manor with Hal and Vanessa who were holding hands.

The grey Mercedes had the top down and Berkley was loading the boot with champagne and two wicker hampers containing our evening meal.

"Double date." James smiled at me.

"Excellent." I said and meant it.

As we got into the car I noticed something about Vanessa. It was a thing I had a talent for, used to notice with my secretaries when I was a work.

They could never hide it from me, and usually as soon as I saw it I found some reason to sack them.

Vanessa's tummy had a slight protrusion under the navel, tilted forward slightly.

"You're pregnant." I heard myself saying out loud.

"Good God," Vanessa laughed,"how did you know?"

"You've changed shape." I smiled embarrassed.

"Congratulations." James laughed shaking Hal's hand. "When?"

"About Christmas time, I'm only about 14 weeks." Vanessa spoke for him.

I really must stop and think before I speak, I thought to myself.

"Bloody inconvienient – what with all the celebrations at the Hotel." she smiled at Hal.

"It'll be fine." he squeezed her hand.

James took my hand in his and opened the front passenger door for me.

"Thanks Berkley, that's all for now." he waved over my shoulder. I looked round – Berkley waved back, but not I thought at James. Vanessa raised a knowing eyebrow at him and turned in the back seat.

"Well, this is lovely, we haven't done this for an absolute age." she crooned snuggling up to Hal in the back seat.

James parked at the top of the hill behind the castle and he and Hal carried the picnic boxes down the hill so we could sit on the top of Overdown man's head. It was quite steep and slippy, but the view across the valley with the sun going down, was stunning.

Vanessa and I flung the rugs on the dry grass and I sat next to her. I still didn't know what to think of Vanessa, I can usually read people like a book, but not her. She was wearing Gucci sunglasses as a hairband and a peachy coloured floaty dress that reached her ankles. Beside her, I felt dowdy and underdressed, but then I was supposed to be Hilary.

"Are you all right?" she asked, it being her turn to be perceptive.

"I can't help thinking it was Berkley who murdered Mrs Withers."

Vanessa went as white as a sheet. "Good God, I hope not, I've just tried to poach him off James." She gave a brittle little laugh.

"What? What?" James sounded like his father. He and Hal had been trying to set up the picnic stove to put a kettle of bottled water on it.

I was in a strange mood, and thought there was no point in hiding my thoughts from him now.

"I was just saying that I thought it was Berkley who killed Mrs Withers."

I pushed my glasses up my nose a bit. "He had everything to gain."

James frowned at me. I thought he was going to tell me not to be so stupid.

He didn't. When the stove was lit with the kettle hissing away, the salad on the plates and the lettuce blowing away in the breeze, James sat on the rug beside me and took my hand in his. I felt he was going to explain something to me as if I were a child.

Vanessa put her sunglasses over her eyes, but she was watching us closely.

"Berkley tried everything to get Evie back and every time Withers thwarted him." Jame sighed. "He came to the police station to ask for help. I said try a different tack old man, try and make friends with the old bag. He did.

I was a very poor cop then, but I kept an eye on her."

The kettle whistled and Hal made the tea, Earl Grey with a dot of milk. Assuming everyone took tea the way he did, he handed the teas round.

"So?" I was intrigued.

Vanessa took up the tale whilst sipping her tea. "He joined the Morris, he had learned the fiddle at school but could never afford one of his own. So he asked Withers if, when she wasn't available, he could borrow her fiddle to play for us."

"Why did she agree to that?" I stuffed a piece of flyaway lettuce into my mouth as Vanessa continued.

"I think she wanted to keep an eye on him, he tried every way he could to befriend the old bitch and win her over. Finally after six years she signed the release papers for Evie. He had no reason to kill her."

"But I thought he was celebrating at the wake." I sipped my tea.

"Yes, he was – the start of a new life with his wife and child." James smiled.

"Did she do it? Evie I mean."

"No, she was out trying to build her life again, trying to re-connect with her old school friends, in the Wine bar in Underdown, loads of people saw her."

My head was starting to hurt, none of this made sense to me, I'm good at this when I choose to be.

"What on earth possessed her to burn the house down, she was living with Mrs Withers wasn't she?" I looked at my companions who were watching the darkening horizon.

"That was part of her release terms." James put on his sun glasses, "All being well, she would have been with Berkley and Alice in a couple of months."

Hal was obviously sick of the conversation, "The Coroner said it was an accident, Evie had gone bonkers again – fired the house – James's legal team got her off." He glugged his tea, "Now can we PLEASE change the subject?"

"Yes, lets talk about something else." Vanessa agreed, "The Summer ball – are you doing it James or are we?"

I sat hardly listening as they discussed the ball in between mouthfuls of food. I watched as the sky darkened to a navy blue in front of us and the shadow of the castle glowed red in the sunset behind us.

Everyone turned to watch the last vestiges of the red threads of the sun leave the sky. I didn't bring sunglasses like the others. So instead of watching the sun's blood red ball drop behind the castle, I watched their faces.

Hal and Vanessa snuggled together, their faces in profile lit by the gold of the setting sun. They looked like an advert for perfection.

James turned, smiling down at me, putting his arm around my shoulder, squeezing me closer to him.

Perhaps these were not really bad people, did I really need to know what happened to the odious Withers woman? I could let this one go couldn't I?

○◯〜◯

I was lying in bed awake thinking that I had moved to the murder capital of the Cotswolds. Three murders in less than six months. What was worse it all seemed so normal to people around here that there seemed no effort to solve them, as if it happened everyday of the week.

Perhaps I should buy myself a funny little felt hat with felt flowers on it and a grey duster coat like the real Miss Marple and pretend to know nothing when in fact I am the only one who knows everything.

A strong arm pulled me closer to spoon with him.

Talking of Miss Marple - my little tabby cat with the same name - was sitting on the kitchen window cill watching two dogs sleeping in front of the Aga.

Poirot, her big brother, had his small brown and white friend's head laying over his back and they were both snoring.

Missy made a disgusted little eeow noise and turned to see the sunrise over the back garden. The sun lit the apple trees and painted the roses that were now starting to go over with a cool morning light.

I had left the Manor in my car after a peck on the cheek from James and a sort of double kiss, mwah, mwah, from a smug Vanessa and Hal. Although not far to drive, I felt incredibly lonely on the way back home. Wet stuff was pouring from my eyes like a tap turned on. Another new experience for me.

When I got back to the cottage, unable to use the usual crutches of the cyber age – facebook, twitter, texting. I called Adrian to come over.

By the time he arrived it was very late and I was very tearful. He lit the Aga and put a bottle of red wine in front of it so it would warm by the fire.

"It's not like you – this." He sat opposite me and took my hand holding it on the scrubbed pine table. I looked across at him, wiping my eyes with the back of my other hand, realising that my waterproof mascara wasn't.

"What's happening?" he asked kindly.

"I want to go home." I sobbed. "I just don't know where that is anymore."

"Come here." In a moment he was holding me, warm, strong, comforting.

I cried black mascara on his Pringle shirt.

Before either of us knew what was happening we were in my bedroom having passionate comfort sex. Afterwards I felt better and I think so did he. We lay talking for ages afterwards, forehead to forehead. Whispering; which was really silly, as cats and dogs can't gossip, or if they did no-one would understand what they were saying.

My side light was on. I could see his handsome face, aqualine nose, hair outrageously thick and unruly from the sex.

"Tell James you don't want to marry him." He whispered. "He's a big boy, he'll get over it."

"Adrian, before I came here I was a horrible person. I did nasty things without even thinking about the people involved. For me there were no repercussions to anything. I needed to change. I'm trying to change to be good now."

"How does that affect James?" he pulled me closer so we were lips to lips.

I could smell and taste the red wine on his breath.

"You didn't see him that day, when his cold hearted bitch of a mother said the word "No" to him. No, I don't love you. No, I never have. No, you are a nobody and will never be anybody. It cut through him like a knife. Dorcas said so much in one cold word. No."

"But that's not your fault." he kissed the tip of my nose.

"Yes it is." I moved away slightly so I could see his eyes. "I caused it all. I solved the murders when James, who was actually in the police at that time, didn't. I broke his family to bits with it."

"Why do you think he didn't solve them? It wasn't that he couldn't." Adrian brushed my hair off my forehead. "He didn't want to."

"Exactly, I come barging in wanting everything put right, messing it all up."

I sighed, "I can't say no to him yet it'll kill him."

"Then you'll just have to marry him out of pity." Adrian grinned at me. "You do know that stringing him along is just as cruel don't you?"

I smiled but tears were falling softly again.

"He won't die." Adrian was using his comforting grown up smile. "He'll be fine."

I didn't want James to be fine, I wanted him to die of love for me. I didn't want him, but I didn't want anyone else to have him. I was still a horrible person.

"I know this isn't the real thing for you Hilary, and I know this shouldn't have happened between us, but if you want, I can be a friend with benefits as our American cousins call it." He took my hand and kissed my palm. "BUT, if I meet HER, the girl of my dreams, this has to stop, agreed?"

"I'm not a nice person doing this to you." I stroked his hair back into place,

"I don't seem to feel love for anyone. Lust yes, but not love."

"One day Hilary your heart will open, you are part way there, and when it does you'll need floodgates sweetheart."

Then he turned over and fell silently asleep leaving me with my mind racing. I put my hand into my side table drawer and pulled out a black and white ribbon with a knot and a bell on it. After the furore of Mrs Wither's death died down I took Poirot for a walk past her cottage. I'd never seen that end of Overdown and was curious to see where she lived.

I walked down the lane, stopping by the black and yellow police tape across the neatly manicured lawn. At the bottom of the hedge under a sign that said "Police Operation in Progress" lay the distinctive black and white ribbon of the Squire of the Morris.

Bits were always falling off their costumes due to the jumping, skipping and vigorous foot stamping. Vanessa had not noticed and neither had the police, a bit of black and white ribbon caught on the hedge by the gate as she had gone past. A nothing. An everything.

I picked it up in a clean tissue and took it home. I felt in someway that it was my security.

That night at Harding Hall Vanessa looked in on her boys. They were brown from playing cricket in the sun all day and their hair was the lighter for it.

Just like Hal's, she smiled to herself. She was proud of them and wanted to kiss their foreheads.

She knew if she did she'd wake them, so she closed the door softly and walked along the dimly lit corridor to Artemis' room.

She opened the door quietly, but a pair of bright blue eyes met hers.

"Are you all right darling?" she crooned.

"Mother, mummy, has Mrs Withers really gone?" Artemis was clutching her duvet under her chin.

"Yes." Vanessa smiled at her daughter as she stroked her hair.

"Will I have to go to Overdown Primary now – like Paloma?"

"No sweetheart, you'll stay at your school." Vanessa could see she was worried, her little face had almost crumpled ready to cry.

"Just in case she comes back?" Artemis asked.

"She'll never come back." Vanessa lay on the bed beside her daughter.

"She'll never hurt anyone again." She took her in her arms hugging Artemis' skinny little body in the fluffy pink pjs, Vanessa kissed the top of her head.

"Try and get some sleep darling, I have to go to bed now, I'm really tired."

Vanessa got up and passed a well worn blue teddy to Artemis.

"Was it a nice picnic?" asked Artemis playing for time hugging her bear.

"Yes, it was, now go to sleep."

"Do you like the Hilary person mummy, will she be your friend?"

"Artemis you do ask the silliest questions – now go to sleep. Remember what we always say?"

They both spoke together. "Goodnight, sleep tight, don't let the bed bugs bite!"

"Love you Artie." Vanessa smiled as she switched the nightlight on and closed the door.

Vanessa walked along the long gallery at the top of the house. It was quiet apart from the sounds of beams and floorboards contracting and expanding in the heat. She stopped halfway along the corridor to look up at a portrait of Paloma in her favourite sky blue dress with big white sash around her waist. The artist had caught her smile and twinkling eyes, behind which was a shadow that Vanessa had never seen, or taken the time to see.

She gently stroked her little bump as she walked along the partially lit corridor, she kept her palm protectively over her precious cargo.

"You can come back now Paloma." She whispered. "Mummy and her friends have made it safe for you to come home."

She opened her bedroom door. The elegant Georgian room was lit with a warm yellow glow, Hal was lying on the four poster in his pyjama bottoms.

He was reading a car magazine.

"Thought of any names yet? How about Porsche or Mercedes?" he laughed, or if it's a boy Bima or Zodiac?"

"Holly Paloma Harding." Vanessa glared at him.

"It might be a boy." Hal ventured.

"It's not going to be." Nessa smiled at him.

Hal knew better than to argue.

Epilogue

Adrian had gone, Toby had arrived, they missed each other by moments. They must have crossed on the road to Overdown.

I had Missy clambering on my shoulder having jumped off the sink. Toby as usual let himself in.

"Morning missus." he grinned pleased to see me.

"Please don't call me that – makes me sound old." I turned the kettle on.

"I don't know what to call you – boss sounds wrong, Hills dwarling is taken." he laughed imitating James. "What about oi you?"

"Just call me Hilary." I smiled, "What's wrong with that?"

"Sounds too formal." he grinned.

He lay the drawings he'd collected from the architect on my table pinning it down with jars of jam and mugs. Our new project.

As he started to explain the costs and work involved I wondered how much Toby really knew about the Wither's business.

"You're not listening." he complained.

"I am, really I am." I picked up my coffee, "Just need caffiene."

Did he know that Evie burnt the cottage to get rid of evidence but saved the fiddle for Berkley so it looked like he borrowed it as usual?

"So we move these doors and extend this room?"

He nodded.

Did he know that Vanessa or Berkley or both had helped Mrs Withers to her doom?

"Pine or oak doors?" I asked, he was absorbed in the plans and making notes in his scruffy notepad. He pulled out a price list to work it out.

James either knowingly or unknowingly had helped Berkley and Evie to a new life of freedom. Did Toby know this? Darren Berkley was his friend after all.

"When can we start?" I asked putting my cup on the price list.

He moved it.

The only innocent in all of this was Hal – and me.

The cat flap slammed open, Missy strolled in holding a huge concussed racing pigeon in her mouth and dropped it at my feet.

"Pick her up. It's still alive." Toby shouted.

I scooped a struggling Missy up away from her prize. Toby gently lifted the Pigeon and inspected it, he took it outside putting it gently on my stone windowcill.

He then took Missy and shut her in the lounge in case she went after the stunned pigeon again.

"What just happened?" I asked surprised.

"The pigeon's just concussed, it'll fly off when it's recovered." He smiled at me, "That's one of Mr Roberts racing pigeons, he loves them, you don't get it do you?"

"No, what do you mean?"

"Well, any animals that become a nuisance in Overdown tend to disappear."

The pigeon ruffled it's feathers, shook itself and flew off. Toby let Missy out of the living room where she'd been hammering at the base of the door.

"You'll have to watch Missy – she looks like a hunter." Missy shot off back into the garden banging the cat flap door behind her.

It suddenly all made sense.

The Girl in the Louboutin Shoes

Before Long

A previously unpublished short story of Hilary's
life before she came to Overdown

It had been a long time since I was on the shop floor so to
speak. I rarely these days wandered down to the third floor,
but today was one of those days. Armand usually dealt with
this kind of thing he enjoyed it. Me, not so much, I didn't
see the point of rewarding work. My people got paid very
well, if they were good, even better, if they got pregnant or
involved in drugs, they got sacked. But as my second in
command was enjoying yet another honeymoon with yet
another wife, it was left up to me.

The lift door opened into the plush hallway, the receptionist,
Madelaine an immaculately groomed young woman
working at her computer smiled at me. Although I'm pretty

sure I heard her whisper 'bitch' through her clenched perfectly white teeth as I passed.

I smiled, thinking it was a good job she was exceptional at what she did, and I had been called a lot worse. I wandered through the modern open plan offices looking for the half of glass box that held Mary Bowers.

Mary was our Financial Analyst and very good at it too, I walked to pod 32 and saw the red lacquered soles of a pair of rather smart black Louboutins on a pair of slim legs crossed at the ankle.

"Sorry to disturb you, I've got the wrong booth – where has Mary Bowers moved to?" The young woman turned round, she was fair with an efficient modern haircut that was more pretty than boyish, an oval pleasant but unremarkable face. "That's me!" she grinned broadly.

The reliable Mary Bowers I knew had shoulder length uncontrollable frizzy dirty blonde hair which stood out like a dandelion clock after a day working in a room full of computers. She was chubby, and always wore flat black pumps. It was strange really that she carried so much weight as she ran about all over the building refusing to take the lifts to keep herself fit. I think it was also because on the staircase it was quiet, there were good views across London, and it gave her time to think and process "the futures".

"Mary? I can't believe it – you look wonderful." I smiled. She smiled back, it was as if she didn't know who I was. She didn't use my name but treated me like a friend she hadn't seen for years. "Oh I had lots done, but it's all been so worth it." She enthused.

"Well, call Roberto over and we'll get this over with." I smiled.

"Get this over with?" She seemed puzzled.

"Your long service bonus and bottle of Mouton Rothschild," I held the bottle up, a few people looked across and smiled.

"Oh of course, of course, I don't wear my contacts working on the computer anymore, my eyesight has changed, sorry I didn't recognise you." She waved to her fiancee Roberto over at the other side of the office and he quickly made his way across.

The Mary I knew had big black glasses with thick lenses and yet another pair for using on the computer, her extremely handsome Italian fiancee was always terrifically touchy feely with her, even in front of me, embarrassingly. It constantly surprised me what he saw in a dumpy, frizzy haired, flat footed financier.

However, this time he didn't come round to her, he stood back behind the glass frame of Mary's box leaned over it and smiled.

Mary stood up, she seemed taller, but then she was wearing 6inch heeled Louboutins, she took the Champagne and the cheque and said the past ten years had been the happiest of her life. Everyone applauded and as was the custom in our place bought plastic cups from the water cooler to help her drink the Champagne – there was barely a spot for each of them! I refused to join them and made my way back up to my suite of offices, on my way I saw Roberto heading for the lift, he saw me. Then changed direction and headed into the empty conference room with a batch of paper files, which he pretended to sort out.

The lift came and as I listened to the soft jazz playing in the background, I had the annoying feeling that something was wrong, but I didn't know what it was. Oh yes, Mary had only been with us five years, I'm sure she said ten, a mathematical genius couldn't have got that wrong, even if she had a lot of "work" done on her it couldn't make her forget that – could it? Anaesthetic was a funny thing – perhaps it had.

Her achievement had obviously not impressed Roberto, he smiled with dead eyes at Mary, and didn't touch her or share the Champagne, he walked away quickly avoiding me. Jealous perhaps? He'd only been with us for three years.

It was two minutes past five, I rang HR and they had gone home. Part-timers, I hissed to myself taking out my set of skeleton keys to their office. As I came out of the lift and the cleaners were already emptying the bins.

"You – big boss lady." Abeba snarled at me, she was a tall thin Ethiopian woman wearing colourful national dress with a green tabard over the top of it. It had "Quality Cleaners UK" embroidered on it's pocket. "What you do bout smell?"

"Smell?" I asked intrigued, I was used to the rudeness of Abeba and the way she addressed me, it made me smile. "What smell?"

"Drains smell in car park." She stood bin in hand, "What you do?"

"Drains in London always smell Abeba." I walked into the HR office

She put her arm across the door stopping me going through, "What you do?"

"Have you spoken to House Management?" I asked.

"Same as you – drains always smell in London."

"There you are then." I closed the door, she made a clicking noise with her tongue obviously disgusted with me.

I sat on the still warm office chair and pulled up Mary's file, it was a five year bonus. Intrigued, I decided to read Mary's latest annual review, it was surprisingly poor. I looked on her leave chart, Mary had taken days off here and there but no weeks at a time, in fact she'd accumulated over six weeks in back leave. I read her latest sick leave requests, two days over two months, both for migraines.

I stood up and walked to the window, it was getting dark and the traffic was already static on the roads below. Did she have all that work done last year? Really? Surely I would have noticed. When did I last see her? I couldn't remember. My cab was waiting to take me late night shopping, I got my coat, brushed my hair and walked into the underground car park where it was waiting. It really did smell as if the drains were up. I covered my nose with my hankie as I walked to the car. "Harvey Nicholls Knightsbridge." I ordered as I got into the cab.

"Betcha got a body in that drain missus," the cabbie pulled out into the traffic which was starting to thin. "You need to get it sorted before the sewage starts coming up the toilets."

"Thank you for that image Solly." I read his name off his ID card. He swerved to avoid a bike, "You need to get a company in to do it – my brother-in-law is the bloke you need." He threw a card through the half open window when we stopped at the lights.

"Drain-o-matic Dramatic drain clearance." I read aloud "Very original." I said sarcastically, which was lost on him.

"Tell him Solly sent you, he'll give you a deal." He pulled up "Here we are that'll be 15 quid."

I gave him a twenty and he pretended to look for the change.

"Keep it." I said already walking towards a display of Louboutin handbags in the window.

After much conversation with the floor attendant, I managed to get hold of the Store Manager and get her to search for Mary's Louboutin shoes in the records. She couldn't find the name. Perhaps Roberto had bought them for her, she duly looked up Roberto Vacca, but no.

I walked out without buying anything – a first for me, I think one of the attendants fainted in shock!

In the lift up to my flat I turned the card Solly gave me over in my hand, I'd ring tomorrow.

I arrived at the office at 8am, remembering a line from Jane Austen,

"if there was anything disagreeable to do, men were bound to get out of it." I gave a fleeting thought to the silver fox with his wolfish smile, Armand on honeymoon with his eighteen year old new wife and shuddered. Where was he when the shit was about to literally hit the fan?

I called Drain-o-matic and they arrived punctually, London obviously wasn't as bunged up with sewage and dead bodies as Solly had thought. They cordoned off part of the car park and I sent a couple of security men to keep an eye on the proceedings.

I couldn't concentrate all morning, even eating a doughnut out of panic then sicking it up an hour later as I shouldn't have eaten it in the first place. I drank lots of water and brushed my teeth and it was about 12 o'clock when I got a phone call from security asking me to come to the car park.

So Mary was in the sewer.

"It's a big-un alright" Solly's brother-in-law Abe stood over an open pit.

"Don't be so rude, she wasn't that big." I walked towards the hole. "It's paper." I said surprised. "Paper and crap."

"Yes, but look at the paper." Dave the security man hooked out a wet mess with a metal rod from the drain-o-matic lorry,

"It's from our actuary office and the finance department." I held my nose. "Most of it is ruined."

"That's a good thing." Dave's considerable bulk squatted beside the paper, "Because reading this bit, it looks like we're in a lot of trouble."

I screwed my head sideways and took a look. He was right.

After a discussion with Abe, he hosed and destroyed most of the "berg".

"Crapbergs are the most common, then fatbergs, never had a paperberg before."

"Berg?" I enquired innocently.

"Like iceberg." Abe explained hose in hand.

I went into my executive bathroom and took a shower and changed my clothes, the smell of the papercrapberg was all pervading. When spruced up I called my auditors and accountants. Despite what I had read on the disgusting papercrapberg, everything was absolutely fine. There was no financial disaster on the cards.

"Ticketky Boo," said Simon head of everything financial. As they walked back to their offices, I called for Roberto to come and see me. I also called Dave in security to go and box up Roberto's glass cube and take it to reception. My secretary the ever efficient Stephanie knew what was happening and had his references and P45 ready and waiting when he appeared.

Stephanie said he swept out of the office swearing in Italian, thumped her desk making her jump and walked straight into the arms of Dave with the contents of Roberto's glass box in a cardboard box. Dave escorted him out of the building.

I then called for Mary Bowers, she arrived wearing a pair of 6inch heeled black and grey patterned Louboutins with a peep toe as it was dress down Friday.

"I want you to go to our offices in Paris Mary, they have a problem with understanding your latest set of figures." I lied.

"Roberto has been fired?" Her eyes slyly checked out my Louboutins as she changed the subject. I was wearing a pair of red Dorissima red suede sky high heels, painful in the extreme.

"Well anyone who causes me to spend large amounts money because he hasn't enough sense to use the shredder deserves it. What the hell gave him the idea to flush it all down the toilet?" I asked.

"No idea." She looked up at me, "I don't think I can go to Paris today, what if I'm late back? I have no-one to feed my cat."

"Let me put it this way Mary," I leant across my desk menacingly, "If you don't go, your cat will starve anyway, or in a language you can understand, no more Louboutins for you."

"Oh,okay then." She smiled charmingly. "Of course."

"Stephanie has your plane tickets, it'll only take a couple of hours to get there." I stood up wobbling slightly on my sky highs. "I'll expect you back here at around nine tonight to report directly to me.".

I looked at the clock, it was coming up to half past nine already, where did the time go? "Off you go then." I waved her out. I watched her walk away, I had an awful lot to do today, where to start?

It was raining when Mary Bowers appeared in front of Stephanie in my office, her peep toe Louboutins had made her toes black from walking about in the rain, her new raincoat was soaked.

"What a waste of time, they didn't understand a word I said." She took her coat off and put in on the plastic coat stand by the door that looked like outstretched white hands. It always made me smile.

Stephanie smiled, "She won't be long, would you like a coffee?".

"Yes please," Mary sat and Stephanie handed her a tall white cup.

"Send Mary in will you?" I barked through the intercom.

Mary walked through the door of my elegant office with her coffee. It was as if I were having a meeting. A couple of burly well-dressed young men were sitting on the elegant faux 17thCentury French chairs and Stephanie joined us with her note book.

"Well?" I asked, staring at Mary. She smiled flirtaciously at the dark haired young man nearest to her and crossed her legs, hitching her skirt up to do so.

"Waste of time." She sipped her coffee and ran a soft pink tongue over her lips. "I don't know why you sent me there."

"I have a purpose in everything I do." I smiled at her. I threw a set of keys on her desk. "Do you know what these are?"

"Keys." She smiled taking a sip of her coffee.

"Skeleton keys." I corrected her, "they can open any door, they opened your door."

"So?" Mary sat forward, "There's nothing in my office locker I have to be ashamed of."

I smiled,"Oh dear, I didn't go into your locker Mary, I went into your house."

Her face fell and she stood up. "How dare you?" she spat angrily. "Who do you think you are?"

"I know who you are Kimberley, Kimberly White." I stood up. "Stalker, kidnapper, blackmailer."

"You're mad." She stared at me pityingly as if I didn't understand.

"You bet I am." I stared at the burly plain clothes policemen, "Take her out of my sight." I hissed.

"She didn't deserve this life, I DID." Kimberley shouted, "She didn't deserve Roberto, I did. Mary is plain and boring and wears glasses." She made it sound like it was the worst thing in the world.

Earlier that morning when I called Roberto into my office, he sat quietly, sadly, as if he knew he was going to be sacked. "Scusa." he muttered under his breath.

"Nothing to be sorry for Roberto." I said trying to sound kindly, not something I was used to. "That's not Mary is it? She vaguely looks like Mary and sort of sounds like her, but it's not her."

"Shhh, she watches me, she has peoples watching me." The handsome tanned face paled, "If she hears, if she knows.." He stood up ready to run like a frightened rabbit. "The things she will do."

"I'm with you now, Roberto, have you ever seen me run away from trouble?"

"Nessuno." His face relaxed a little.

"This is what we'll do. Dave will stay with you all day, he'll see you home safely and stay with you. Leave the rest to me."

"No, no if he stays she will know, I am watched all the time." Roberto chewed his fingertips. "He mustn't come with me, if I am sacked, I go alone right?"

"You do realise you are not really sacked?" I smiled.

His brown eyes saddened,"Makes no difference to me, I can't be here without amore mio."

I stood up. "It will all be well." I squeezed his hand. "I'll make it happen."

"Now use that anger, shout at me in Italian and don't forget Stephanie on the way out." I squeezed his arm, "fidati di me."

So that is what he did. He trusted me.

I was rather glad he hadn't claimed Dave for the day because I needed him, he drove me to a rather handsome Edwardian house in Rosebery Avenue in Finchley. The door was beautiful with stained glass lilies in the top panels.

It was obviously two flats, Dave turned the skeleton key and opened the mortis lock, and one good shove of his shoulder opened the yale.

The hallway had two doors within it, one obviously led upstairs, but it was the downstairs flat we were interested in. Another turn of the skeleton key and a shove on the Yale and we were in. There was a long hallway with a patterned red rug along it, all the walls were painted white. I opened the first door we came to – a small tidy kitchen leading by a side door into the garden. The next door was a surprise, a huge bedroom with glossy fitted wardrobes on remote control, I opened the doors with the remote consumed with noseyness. There in rows were every kind of Louboutin shoe imaginable, nearly everything from this years range, all with the trademark red sole. Platforms, peep toes, narrow toed pumps with six inch heels, ankle straps, about 200 of them in all.

Dave opened the door to the bathroom, black and silver, tasteless I thought. "This is useless." He moaned. Then we heard it, a banging noise coming from what looked like a cupboard, we opened it to find it was a door to a small office just behind the kitchen, at one time it would have been the larder.

Sitting in the semi darkness, chained hand and foot to the desk was Mary Bowers, her mouth covered with silver gaffer tape. I pulled it off as gently as I could. Dave was on his mobile to the police. Mary was sobbing.

"Oh thank God, thank God." She was shaking as I tried the skeleton keys on her padlocks, they didn't work. "Desk" she said hoarsely. I looked at a small desk in the corner- the keys hung on a hook screwed into the side of it. I turned the keys in the handcuffs she was wearing, her wrists were red raw and blistering, Mary hugged me ferociously,

"I knew you'd find me." I released her feet from the chains just as the police arrived, two burly plain clothes men and a woman.

"We'll take over now." the policewoman snapped.

Mary had lost weight, her hair was greasy and lank, she had bruises and cigarette burns across her arms and legs.

Out in the daylight her face was pale, and she had red marks across her mouth where the gaffer tape had silenced her. She stared myopically into the street. "Is she here?"

"No, I sent her to the Paris office." I put my arm around Mary, but the policewoman pushed me off. Poor Mary smelt of urine and sweat and had no shoes, as I looked at her bare feet I realised why she never wore high heels to work, she was completely flat footed.

"Come now." The Policewoman took Mary's hand.

"Where are you taking her?" I asked.

"Barnet General to get her patched up." The ponytailed policewoman smiled, "Do you want to come?"

"Take her to my man at the London, come with us." I pulled myself up to my full height. "Don't say you can't – say you can."

"Out of our area." She said brusquely. "Barnet is nearer, she needs help now." pushing Mary into the car.

I got in beside Mary in the car aware that my new suit would need cleaning immediately that I got home, she held my hand tightly. Not something I liked but it seemed important to her.

"Don't ring Roberto, she'll know, she'll kill him." Mary sobbed.

"Who's Roberto?" Asked the policewoman kindly.

"My fiancee." Mary sobbed, "She has him watched all the time."

"I sent her to Paris for the day, she's out of touch. Roberto is safe, he's at home." I tried to comfort Mary as we drove up Barnet hill to the hospital.

"Oh God, oh God, he's not safe, if she finds out, she'll have him killed."

"You mind me saying something here?" Policewoman Weir smiled, "This is a well known physcological trick, she probably watches Roberto now and then, enough to keep his guard up. You are watching yourselves for her."

Mary's mouth worked as if she was going to say something.

"Do you want me to ring Dave to go fetch him here?" I asked.

"Who's Dave?" asked Policewoman Weir.

"My Chief of Security." I answered. "He called you to the house."

"And who are you?" She asked.

I told her.

"Oh my God." The policewoman grinned, "I never thought I'd have someone like you in my squad car."

I sat in a dingy hospital corridor for what seemed like hours while Mary was examined and photographed. It was getting on for two o'clock when Roberto arrived with Dave.

"Where is amore mio?" Roberto had a small case of clothes for Mary, "Is she safe?"

"She's being patched up, photographed, and God knows what else." I beckoned Roberto to sit beside me. "What the hell is all this about?"

Roberto put his head in his hands and sobbed with relief. "I will tell you, I will," he took a breath and reached into the pocket of his Armani suit and pulled out a photograph.

Mary and Kimberley sat side by side on a park bench looking very young and very alike.

"They were friends at school, often taken as sisters, they lost touch, years passed, and when we decided to get married Mary wanted her best friend from school to come." He took a huge breath and sobbed, "Abbiano cercato quel demone."

"What?" asked Dave.

"They searched for that demon." I whispered to Dave.

"As soon as we met, it was if they had never been apart. Mary was so happy." Roberto looked up, Mary was showered, her hair was wet, and she approached us smiling wearing a hospital gown, with arms outstretched to Roberto.

"What did she do to you mio amore?" He showered her with kisses. "I have some clothes for you and your spare occhiali." Mary searched through the little case and put her glasses on. "Grazie mia cara." she smiled at him. They were shown into a room where Mary could get dressed, Roberto followed her in.

"So this Kimberley White started stalking Mary," Policewoman Weir took up the story, "Watched her every move, copied everything she did, got to the point where she was more Mary than Mary, tried to take Roberto away from her, but that was never likely to happen, so decided to make them pay."

"How did my company get involved in all this?" I asked, but Dave took up the story, "Mary did the same work as she always did, but from Kimberley's house, while she went to work pretending to be Mary." Dave smiled, "Mary was a clever little girl, she tried to make big mistakes to make someone notice there was something wrong with the paperwork."

"What went wrong?" I asked puzzled, "Why didn't we notice?"

"Because il ratto Kimberley always asked a colleague to countersign the work." Roberto appeared, "When she realised what we were doing, she made me get rid of it, I thought if I put it into il bagno, it would how you say stuff up? And it would be found out." Mary appeared, made up, foundation hiding the marks around her mouth, wearing with her big black glasses and bright red lipstick.

"It worked, he so clever." Mary smiled at Roberto and you could feel the electricity in the air. So this was love. Real love.

"Not all of the work was bad," Mary smiled, "Some was just average. I was punished for trying to do bad work. She pulled up her sleeve, her arm was covered in cigarette burn holes, red and sore, covered with a transparent hospital dressing.

Even my big brave Chief of Security blenched seeing it. "How long did this go on for?" He asked.

"About eight weeks I think." Mary hugged into Roberto, "Seemed like forever. She told me she was going to kill me and take my six weeks holiday with Roberto, and he had to do as she said to keep me alive, but I wouldn't be alive, and he would fall in love with her."

"Delusional." I said shocked. "I think Dave should take you to the Savoy tonight, unless you want to go home."

They looked at one another "Savoy." They said simultaneously.

I booked a cab to take me back to Knightsbridge, strangely it was Solly.

"Hear the berg wasn't a body." He said smiling.

"No." I picked up my phone it was ringing, it was Armand.

"Anything new?" he asked.

"Same old, same old." I answered.

"So you're bored?" He asked.

"Not exactly, but I think we need to open an office in Milan and I have just the people to do it."

ABOUT THE AUTHOR

Margaret Cooper Evans was born in Shoreditch in London. She started writing for pocket money at the age of 14 for teenage magazines and has had articles published in national newspapers & short stories in women's magazines.

She worked in the BBC as a video graphics operator, camera operator and News 24 Media Manager.

After being made redundant she turned to her second love and became a historical re-enactor, living history interpreter and a speaker on the lives of women in the 17th Century. She joined The Sealed Knot re-enactment society in 1996. Since then she has played the part of a Baggage Woman, a Musketeer, a Housekeeper, a Lady and a Farmers Wife in the Living History encampment. Twenty years of research culminated in her first factual History book; **The Women of the English Civil War**. Margaret makes 17th Century clothing and also cooks authentic 17th Century food.

She became a professional author in 2012 and working in Stately Homes for the National Trust gave her the idea for the successful Hilary Long Mysteries series of short novellas. She currently lives in the Cotswolds with her husband and two cats.

Coming soon to paperback

The Collected Hilary Long Mysteries: Part 2
featuring

Christmas in Overdown
Man Down in Overdown
The Girl in the Red Shirt *(previously unpublished)*

The Collected Hilary Long Mysteries: Part 3

featuring

Halloween in Overdown
Murder in Overdown Manor
Norwegian Blood *(previously unpublished)*

*All Hilary Long stories are also available on Amazon
Kindle including*

Evil in Overdown

Also available in Paperback

1955

a vintage murder mystery

The Women of the English Civil War

The true stories of womens lives in 17ᵗʰ C England